SCAREDY CAT, SCAREDY CAT

Phil Earle

SCAREDY CAT, SCAREDY CAT

Illustrated by Sara Ogilvie

Orion
Children's Books

ORION CHILDREN'S BOOKS

First published in Great Britain in 2017 by Hodder and Stoughton

1 3 5 7 9 10 8 6 4 2

A CIP catalogue record for this book
is available from the British Library.

ISBN 978 1 4440 1393 1

Printed and bound in Great Britain by Clays Ltd, St Ives plc

The paper and board used in this book are from well-managed forests
and other responsible sources.

MIX
Paper from
responsible sources
FSC® C104740
www.fsc.org

Orion Children's Books
An imprint of
Hachette Children's Group
Part of Hodder and Stoughton
Carmelite House
50 Victoria Embankment
London EC4Y 0DZ

An Hachette UK Company
www.hachette.co.uk

www.philearle.com
@philearle
www.facebook.com/PhilEarleAuthor
www.hachettechildrens.co.uk

This book is dedicated to the fearless
and utterly fabulous Kay Packwood
P.E.

For Dani, Holger & Sita
S.O.

Liv

Daisy

A cat

Grumblemore

If I was to say the word 'wizard' to you, what would pop into your head?

An old man, maybe, with a face wizened by generations of fighting evil.

He might have a long white beard, possibly plaited. He might be wearing half-moon spectacles and a long pointy hat, complete with matching gown.

He might be accompanied by a cat.

You might not have thought any of these things, of course. Some of you would probably just tut, irritated at being pulled away from your Xbox to be asked such a ridiculous question.

I mean, wizards. What a tiresome thought.

Wizards are the stuff of fiction; they belong in dusty old paperback books, or far-fetched films that last longer than a Saharan summer.

But what if I told you that old men like this really do exist?

In real life.

That there *are* ancient people out there who can make magical things happen, and change the fortunes of others.

Would you believe me? Would you come along for the ride as I described what happened with one such old man and a timid, fearful girl in the crumbly seaside town of Seacross?

You would? That's excellent news.

Well, grab yourself a biscuit, plump up your cushion, and let me tell you the tale of the Storey Street Sorcerer and one very Scaredy Catt . . .

Kay Catt, Scaredy Catt, Don't Know What She's Looking At

Kay Catt awoke with a start.

She hadn't had a bad dream; she always woke up that way. Nervously.

The first thing that crossed her mind as her eyes flew open was 'AAAAAARRRGGHHHH! There's something in my bed! I can feel it touching my hand.'

Her body went rigid, her mind cartwheeling with fear.

What was it? What was it? *What?*

A burglar perhaps? Or a hopelessly lost – and bitey – Amazonian beast?

It was neither. Believe me.

There *was* something in her bed, and it *was* touching her hand, but it wasn't a sneaky thief or a wild animal. Not unless you class a ten-year-old stuffed otter called Fluffy-Poo as a predator.

'Fluffy-Poo!' Kay shrieked. 'Why would you scare me like that?'

If ageing stuffed otters with overly cute names could speak, they'd defend themselves, and Fluffy-Poo would tell Kay that he hadn't done it on purpose. He was in the same place he was every night, because if he wasn't by Kay's side, she struggled to sleep.

It summed our hero up, though. Kay Catt was . . . jumpy. Jumpier than a bunch of clockwork frogs doing their best kangaroo impressions whilst playing on a trampoline.

The second shock of the day came as soon as her feet hit the floorboards.

'AAARRRGGGH!' she yelled again, the surprise of the cold planks whacking the DISTRESS button in her brain. She scuttled towards her slippers on the far side of the room. But as her pinkies galloped across the floor, she passed the mirror, spotting a sight that filled her veins with ice.

A girl! In her room! With the most terrifying bird's-nest hair and crusted eye-bogeys.

Kay threw her hands to her face, not daring to look, but her breathing sounded so terrifyingly echoey inside her hands that she dropped them – only to see the girl once more, eyes wide and staring.

This prompted a bizarre cycle of the whole 'hands to face – loud breath – hands down' routine, which only ended when Kay realised that the girl in the mirror was actually *her*, and her heartbeat dropped to its normal rate of one hundred and twenty-six beats per minute.

Oh, dear readers, it makes my heart splinter to see Kay like this.

It might seem to you that she's more unhinged than a rotten stable door, but I promise you she's not. She's a brave one, is Kay: you'll see that as the story goes on.

After another minute of mild scares and severe paranoia, Kay gathered herself enough to make the trip to the bathroom, overcoming such terrifying perils as the slightly frayed hall carpet and the bannister that looked like it might splinter some time in the next thirty-seven years.

But as she neared the bathroom door, she paused, as she always did, by a framed photograph at the top of the stairs.

The photo was as daring as Kay was timid, as in it were three figures on top of a huge snow-capped mountain: a man, a woman and a small child, no older than two years old. The child was strapped to the woman's back in a rucksack, and all three of them were connected to a series of climbing ropes.

It was clear they were standing somewhere really, really high – so high they could've been wearing spacesuits instead of ski jackets.

The most amazing thing about the photo, though, was the joy radiating from all three of them. With their arms punching the air and smiles as vast as the Alps, they looked like they'd won the lottery, on Christmas day, which also happened to be their birthdays.

Kay looked at the photo as she always did, and gulped, as she always did. Then she sweated and felt a bit dizzy, knowing that the wee girl in the rucksack was her, and the other two people were Dad, and Mum.

But she didn't let herself finish the thought. Instead she dashed into the bathroom and forced herself to worry about something else, like being eaten alive by the teeny tiny spider that occasionally resided inside the shower curtain.

It was much better to worry about that than think about the lovely, smiley, fearless lady in the photograph.

Twenty minutes and thirty-two scares later, Kay was at the breakfast table, ladling rice crispies into her cereal bowl.

'Don't put too many in your mouth at once,' said a voice, coming down the stairs. 'Small mouthfuls, chewed thirty times, mean a seventy per cent reduction in the possibility of choking.'

Kay looked at her dad, Arthur, and nodded obediently, even though he said the same thing every mealtime.

Kay *always* ate rice crispies for breakfast. They were a safe cereal. Small, round, the explosions they made when you added milk weren't loud enough to damage her eardrums, and after a few minutes they were left soggy.

Kay very occasionally wondered about eating something else, something exotic, like toast . . . or cornflakes. But she knew better than to ask for such delicacies again.

'Toast?' Dad would yelp. 'I don't think you need to be handling butter knives at your age . . . and as for cornflakes? Sharp as razor blades, those things. Deathtraps!'

Nope. She was best off with crispies. No lives would be lost whilst eating them.

Which made both father and daughter feel a lot less anxious.

The pair ambled through their breakfast, Kay sipping diluted orange juice from an unbreakable plastic beaker whilst Dad drank coffee, which he'd cooled down for safety's sake with a couple of ice cubes.

'What are you doing at school today, sweetheart?' he asked.

'Er, Maths, I think, and English . . . oh, and PE.'

'PE?' Arthur's tone carried more than a hint of worry. 'What kind of PE?'

'Oh, you know. Jumping over stuff and climbing up ropes.'

'I'll write you a note.'

'A note? What for?' Kay asked.

'So you don't have to do it. I'll say you've got earache or something.'

'But I don't climb the rope with my ears. I use my hands.'

'That's irrelevant. What if you're good at it and reach the top, only to fall? I bet the crash mats underneath won't be anything like thick enough. Plus the rope is probably covered in germs from the other kids' hands. Before you know it you'll have that avian flu and it'll be the quarantine ward in hospital for you.'

Kay didn't like the sound of that. Not one bit. It made her pores gush like a power shower. So much so that she reached inside her bag for some paper and a pen. The sooner she had that note, the better she would feel.

As Dad scribbled, Kay turned back to her sloppy crispies. 'What are you up to today, Dad? Busy?'

'Phenomenally,' he replied with a smile. 'Business is booming. And it's *so* rewarding. Much more so than the old job.'

Arthur ran his own business, one that fitted his worrisome personality perfectly. It was called You Can't Be Too Careful Nowadays and it specialised in gadgets for those of a nervous disposition. House alarms, personal alarms, car alarms, pepper spray, bubble wrap – if you wanted a safe, anxiety-free life, then Arthur could sell you it.

It was a far cry from the company he owned before with Mum.

Wildest Dreams had been their pride and joy, selling the toughest, most durable mountain-climbing ropes ever seen anywhere in the world. You could hang an elephant holding a suitcase full of gold bullion off one of them and it wouldn't so much as fray. But after Mum's accident . . . Well, Dad took the ropes off sale, locked them in the attic and refused to sell one ever again.

Since he started his new venture, he had never been happier. Kay knew this because he told her so every day.

'You know what, my love? Ever since I closed the old business' – he couldn't even bear to say its name – 'I've never been happier. Did I ever tell you that?'

'That's great, Dad,' she replied. How lucky she was to have a dad who was both happy *and* safe. 'I'd better get off to school.'

Dad's eyes flashed with worry as he leapt from his seat to follow her.

'Have you got your phone?' he asked.

'I have.'

'Good. Keep it charged and text me when you get to the school gates.'

'Will do.'

'And at lunchtime.'

'OK.'

'And when the bell rings at three o'clock . . . and when you get out of the gates.'

By the time Kay got her shoes on, she was under no doubt that something awful *was* going to happen to her at school. If Dad was so worried, then it had to be true.

'See you tonight,' she said, and they hugged, Dad squeezing her that bit too hard, like he was never going to see her again.

'I'll be back from work then and waiting.'

He would as well. He'd be on the front step, wringing his hands until she appeared. Only when she got through the front door and he locked it behind her would either of them be able to relax. A bit.

Slowly, Kay pulled away from her dad, opened the front door and took a deep breath. Then, and only then, did she dare to step outside into the Storey Street sunshine.

What a Good Place to Be . . .

Storey Street was a wonderful place to live.

It might not have looked like much with its ragbag mixture of crumbly old terraced houses and boxy semi-detacheds, but these homes were full of the most fascinating people.

So many good eggs lived on that street, you could've made a human omelette that would feed an army of ogres for days.

Despite this, Kay felt on the fringes of life there. She never quite felt brave enough to allow herself to be anyone's friend.

This morning was a perfect example. Once outside, Kay pulled a small, knobbly twig from her coat pocket before edging her way to the front gate, eyes flitting nervously up and down the street. She walked with such hesitancy she looked like a goldfish who'd swum into a piranha tank by mistake.

'Hi Kay!' came two voices from behind her, making her almost leap out of her shoes.

It was the twins, Liv and Daisy Smith. Identical, they were. Completely. In looks and thoughts. Even when they spoke, as Daisy would start a sentence and Liv would finish it.

'How are you . . .' Daisy said.

'. . . doing, Kay?' Liv added.

Kay felt nervous, legs buzzing with anxiety. Why were they asking her that? Did she look ill? Did she have a rash or spots? She started to rummage in her bag for a mirror to check, which prompted a confused look from the twins.

'Are you OK? What are you . . . looking for in your bag?'

Kay didn't answer. With a twig in her hand it was hard to search for anything.

'Can we hold that . . . for you?'

Kay held on tight to the twig. No *way* was she letting go of that. Not for them or anyone.

'What do you need it for, anyway? Are you one of those water diviners?' Daisy gasped excitedly.

Liv squealed, 'Can you find a hidden river with a bit of dead wood?'

Kay wanted to shake her head, but didn't dare. She didn't want to get into a conversation about the thing in her hand. You see, Kay wasn't looking for water. Nor was she about to play tennis with the world's rubbishest racket.

The thing in her hand wasn't a twig at all. It was a *wand*.

Kay didn't think she had special powers. She wasn't a nutter, regardless of what anyone thought. She was just a bit obsessed with wizards.

It had started when everything had gone wrong: when Mum died, when Dad gave up his Wildest Dreams, when everything became a bit too scary.

One day, when she couldn't have felt any lower, Kay took refuge in front of the telly to find it playing a film filled with old, bearded men in long, flowing gowns.

For the next three hours these pensioners waved their wands, righting wrongs, fighting evil and being properly powerful and fabulous.

Kay fell in love.

Imagine, she thought.

Imagine being able to sort out everything that was wrong with the world with a flick of your wrist. Imagine being that powerful!

Kay *loved* the idea.

It could be argued, I suppose, that for a girl who was scared of *everything*, all-powerful sorcerers should have been the last people for her to find solace in.

But these wizards' powers were so removed from her reality that she was entranced by them, not scared.

Kay stared at her wand, failing to hear the twins as they walked away, defeated.

'Why won't she . . . ever talk to us?' they asked each other with a sigh, leaving Kay to her thoughts of sorcery.

It occupied her thoughts a lot. If there was a film with a wizard in it, Kay would watch it. If there was a book with one in, she would read it hungrily, again and again, until the pages fell out and she stuck them back together with endless sellotape and lashings of hope.

That's where the wand came in. She'd found it lying in the front garden one morning: it had fallen from a tree she and Mum had planted together. It felt like it had been left there for her on purpose, like a present from Mum, and from that moment on, when out in public, Kay carried it with her. Whenever she felt scared or overwhelmed, she'd wave it subtly and whisper a spell of her own. She didn't do it to hurt anyone, no no no – just to make herself feel better, calmer, safer.

'Nettlerash-aramus!' she'd whisper at dogs who walked by her, growling angrily at something completely unrelated.

'Accio-itchybum!' she'd chant, at the sight of Saliva Shreeve and Bunions Bootle, the street's bully boys, as soon as they even glanced in her direction.

It was moments like this, when she allowed herself to feel even a teeny bit braver and more powerful, that she felt briefly like a ten-year-old girl-wizard rather than a seventy-year-old biddy with the weight of the world on her shoulders.

As she neared the school gates, Kay had to slow down. This wasn't uncommon; there was always a bit of a traffic jam as bell time approached, but today was especially slow, like a colossal mutant slug had stopped for a nap across the entire width of Storey Street.

On the other side of the road, Saliva Shreeve and Bunions Bootle were whooping and hollering at someone, and they were being so raucous about it that the rest of the street had stopped to see what was so funny. What it was, Kay had no idea, or interest. She knew what it was like to be stared at, and had no desire to join in.

Instead, she tucked her wand up her sleeve, leaving only the tip visible, and tried to gently weave her way through the crowd. As she beavered onwards, she continued to cast her spells at the bully boys: bogeys the size of beer barrels for Saliva Shreeve, and premature hair loss for Bunions Bootle. That'd teach them for mocking whoever it was across the road.

But as Kay reached the head of the scrum, curiosity got the better of her.

There, on the other side of the street, stood an old man, surrounded by half a dozen tatty brown boxes.

Big deal, you might think.

Yawnsville, Arizona.

I mean, old people are everywhere, aren't they? Getting in your way as you career down the street at a hundred miles per hour on your scooter, slowing you down in shops as they count out all their pennies to buy one measly packet of sherbet lemons.

But this man – well, he was different. He wasn't sucking a fruity sweet for starters, though his legs moved like your typical old codger, stiffly and slowly, like his joints had been put in a vice and welded shut with a blowtorch. At the same time, though, he was managing to move the boxes around him, and they looked very heavy. He balanced one in one hand almost effortlessly, completely at odds with his tiny, hesitant steps. *Weird*, thought Kay: the box almost looked like it was floating in mid-air.

No one else seemed to notice but Kay, though. Everyone else was too fixated on his clothes. While most old men might wear a pair of bottle green cords and a cardigan complete with leather-patched elbows, this gent was swathed in a long, silky cloak, tied neatly in a bow around his neck.

Kay couldn't take her eyes off it. In fact, she was so entranced that for a second or two she clean forgot to feel scared at the sight of it. One second the cloak was the deepest emerald green, only for it to shimmer with his next step and become a radiant ruby red. It looked magical.

What and how and why? she thought to herself, not daring to blink in case it all turned out to be some sort of apparition.

Her eyes zoomed across the rest of him: the black boots that curled impossibly at the toes like a pair of liquorice yo-yos; the

gnarled, twisted staff that looked like a longer version of
the wand that she clutched in her mitt; the empty
velvet sack slung over his shoulder, and
finally, the hat that sat jauntily upon
his head.

How do I describe
the hat? How do I do
it any kind of justice,
when it was the
strangest thing ever
seen on someone's
head (apart from
the man who wore
a seagull on his
bonce and called
himself Cliff)?

Imagine a traffic
cone, then imagine
that it's made

out of glorious silk patches rather than plastic, then imagine
that someone has bent it in the middle so it's shaped like an
arrowhead.

If you've any imagination left, then picture it sitting jauntily on top of the old man's long grey hair, more proud than a Frenchman's beret as he goes to market to buy a baguette and some stinky cheese.

It's true, yes, it looked ridiculous – how could it not with the rest of his outfit? But at the same time, it suited him. It looked like he'd been born wearing it. It matched the eyes (one blue, one green) that sat behind a pair of half-moon spectacles, and the long beard that had been twisted and coaxed into a braid that reached his waist.

Bemusement, bafflement and the odd 'BA-HA-HA!' bounced around the street, but Kay was oblivious to it. It was like someone had blown a hole in the side of her TV while she was watching one of her favourite films, allowing the very people that had populated her imagination to walk amongst her.

She couldn't believe what she was seeing. She stared and stared until all the boxes had been carried inside by the old man, until he finally emerged from his front door one last time and noticed the crowd watching him.

He didn't appear angry to be the centre of attention, more delighted and amused. He smiled widely, before squinting up at the sky, which looked suddenly heavy and dark.

'Heavens above!' he chanted loudly, and without warning, he lifted his staff from the ground before slamming it down upon his doorstep.

At that point – at the very moment of impact – the sky opened and torrential rain fell like spears, striking at the crowd, forcing them to dash for shelter.

For Kay, it confirmed everything she had been thinking, and although she found herself swept up by the masses, she managed to look over her shoulder for long enough to know that it was true. All of it.

There was a *wizard* living on Storey Street, and Kay didn't know whether to be overwhelmingly excited . . . or utterly, utterly terrified.

Izzy Wizzy, Let's Get Busy

Kay Catt was a smart cookie.

'You get it off your mum,' Dad always told her, though Kay had no idea if that was really true. Mum had died before Kay's brain could squirrel away any precious nuts of memories. Mum only existed to her in the photo at the top of the stairs. Anything else she knew about her came only from her daydreams: from how she imagined she would be. Beautiful, daring, courageous – everything she wasn't.

Now, Kay might have been a Scaredy Catt, but she was also bright and hard-working. Not in a swotty way, though. She wasn't one of those irritating kids who'd respond to a teacher's question by straining so hard with her hand in the air that you thought they'd either die with the effort or let rip with the world's biggest fart.

If a teacher gave her work, she just got on with it, mainly

because it took her mind off all the other stuff in her head that scared her.

The only subject she didn't excel at was Art. She never liked working with sharp pencils in case she accidentally stabbed herself in the heart and contracted lead poisoning.

Lessons today, though, were proving more challenging than eating soup with chopsticks. No matter how hard she tried, Kay couldn't concentrate. All she could think about was the old man.

Had she really seen what she thought she had? And if she had, then what did it mean? Could he really be an all-powerful warlock, or was he just a non-powerful wally?

Saliva and Bunions were under no illusions.

'Did you see that old geezer on the street earlier?' guffawed Bunions.

'What, the pound shop wizard?' said Saliva.

'Careful what you say,' whispered Errol Russo, trying not to laugh. 'Wizards have powerful hearing. He could turn you into a frog in an instant.'

'You what?' said Bunions. 'I doubt he could turn a *TV* over.'

'Turned my stomach, he did,' added Saliva. 'Did you see the length of his beard? Cost him a fortune in shampoo . . . if he ever decided to wash it.'

Kay felt her pulse quicken. She wanted to dive in to their conversation and ask them who he was, where he'd come from, and whether anyone had ever seen him before. The questions backed up in her head like cars in a traffic jam, and her car seemed to have its handbrake on. She didn't dare ask them a thing.

Instead, she tried to picture all the wizards from her favourite books and films, listing all the things about them that could prove the stranger she saw this morning was not one of them. But every time she added another detail, all she could do was put a tick next to it.

Cloak ✔

Hair ✔

Staff ✔

Glasses ✔

Age ✔

If a picture of this mystery man was held up next to one of Gandalf the Grey, anyone with two eyes and a smidgeon of sanity would have insisted they were twins.

It felt like a woodpecker had taken up residence in Kay's chest, causing her insides to fill up entirely with sawdust and making everything decidedly blurry. All she could do to stop being overwhelmed was try and listen again to the conversations around her.

'Bit weird though, isn't it? Walking down the street like that, when Halloween is months away.'

'Maybe he's one of them kissograms, off to snog a granny for her birthday.'

'EUUUUGHHHH!'

'I can't believe he lives on our street. Imagine the smoke that'll be coming off his cauldron!'

'We should follow him next time we see him. Persuade him to make us something we can set off in class. Something that really stinks.'

'Miss Maybury already does that! No one would notice the difference.'

Cue much hilarity and more deep thought from Kay, as the bullies had given her something to ponder. Not that she could believe she was really considering it.

Bunions and Co. might have been joking about following him, but maybe *she* should? The only way she'd know for sure who or what he was, would be to watch him.

She shook the thought from her head. *What are you doing?* she demanded of herself.

Why are you interested? Even if he is a wizard, which he clearly isn't, well, you shouldn't be going within a country mile of him. He's probably just a dotty old codger with a mushroom instead of a brain.

Either way, he clearly wasn't the sort of person she should be mixing with.

Danger wafted from him like garlic off bread. She would be crazy to go anywhere near him. She should go home, lock the door, and pull the duvet firmly over her head.

Just as she did every day.

The thought reassured her, calmed her, whispered in her ear that everything was going to be just fine.

For now at least.

Every Breath You Take...

The bell rang to mark a blissful end to the school day, and after waiting for the rush to die down, Kay edged her way to the gates. No sooner had her big toe hit Storey Street than her phone pinged in her pocket. She didn't need to look to know who the message was from, or what it said.

It was Dad:

Have u left school yet?

He sent the same message every day at 3.10 p.m. and would ring her sixty seconds later if she didn't reply.

Not wanting to hear his panicky voice when her head was already full to brimming, Kay hammered out a reply:

Just. Home in two minutes, fifteen seconds.

As the message flew, Kay let out a sigh of relief. She loved her dad, more than a sumo wrestler loves all-you-can-eat buffets. How lucky was she that he was always looking out for her, always with her safety at heart?

No sooner had she cleared the shadow of school than her phone beeped again.

Dad. AGAIN.

I've had to go to post office. Emergency order for reflective safety underpants for wannabe superhero. Back soon. Do not touch cooker, toaster, dishwasher.

Kay nodded. Made sense. No knowing what could happen if she dared to make herself a toasted sarnie. Her phone pinged again.

Or tumble dryer, TV, radio . . .

Her phone pinged a third time.

Or lights. Oh and don't trap your fingers when you close the front door.

Kay motored towards home, not wanting to get caught in the dark. The sun would be setting in a couple of hours.

But as she reached her front gate, her pulse began to sprint. Walking toward her on the path, no more than twenty paces away, was the mysterious old man.

Kay stopped dead. Her heart thudded, begging her ribcage to part so it could get through the front door safely.

But Kay's feet seemed to be operating on a different, incompatible frequency and wouldn't budge. Even as the old man edged closer, and the dangers of being kidnapped or bewitched by him intensified, still they remained planted.

Within seconds she was sweating heavily. Seconds later it felt like she'd been swimming breaststroke around Niagara Falls (not that she'd go within a continent of such a dangerous, beautiful landmark).

With her feet on holiday, how on earth was she going to escape?

Her mind whirled and her pores opened further, and as the man tottered within half a metre of her, her brain did the only thing it could. It begged for mercy.

'DON'T TURN ME INTO A TOAD!' she yelled, stopping the old codger in his tracks, which took as much effort as it did for him to walk.

He looked shocked, surprised, as if there was someone behind him that Kay was *actually* speaking to. But as realisation dawned that this statement was aimed at him, he fixed Kay with a smile, and his wrinkles relaxed, making him look much younger, perhaps only one hundred and six years old.

'A toad?' he answered, his voice like a mad professor being played through a crackly gramophone. 'A toad? Oh my dear old thing, no, no, no, no, no! If I was to turn you into anything, it wouldn't be a toad. It would be something more befitting of your character, your spirit!' He peered at her over his half-moon specs, his different coloured eyes casting a hypnotic spell.

'Mountain lion!' he yelled suddenly, like it was the secret to eternal life. 'I'd turn you into a mountain lion. Obvious when you think about. Should've seen it much quicker. Sorry about that.'

He lifted his cane from the floor and, hand shaking with the effort, pointed it at Kay's head, causing her to drop to her knees and hide behind the gate. He'd brought on a storm this morning with a mere wave of his staff and she didn't want to be a mountain lion!

Why didn't I just rush inside when I saw him coming? she thought.

But just when Kay expected to see her hands morphing into paws . . . well, they didn't. They remained the same trembling pinkies they always were, and she dared to peek through them, up at the old man, who wore a quizzical expression.

'Absolutely fascinating specimen, you are,' he said. 'Definitely a mountain lion. But perhaps not yet. Soon . . . but not yet. Toodle-pip!'

And with that, he tottered on, the sack upon his back. It was the same velvet one she'd seen that morning, with one noticeable difference.

That morning it was empty and motionless, but now it was bulging. And more than that, it was moving too. Kay gulped. If she was a mountain lion, who *knew* what was struggling inside his bag?

It was time for a lie-down, she thought, as she stepped inside the house.

Doctor in the House

By the time Dad burst through the front door from his intrepid and fraught post office expedition, Kay was slumped on the settee with a wet flannel draped over her head.

'Oh my giddy aunt, what's happened?' he wailed upon seeing her. 'I knew I shouldn't have gone. The post office is just too far away!'

'Da-ad. I'm OK, honest, I'm just having a rest,' Kay replied, though it felt like there was an army of moles burrowing repeatedly against her ribcage.

But Dad wasn't listening. Course he wasn't. He was on his knees, thrusting his emergency thermometer into Kay's mouth.

'Do you feel sick?' he gabbled. 'Any rashes? Nausea? Anything broken?'

'Nggghhhhhhnnnnn,' Kay replied apologetically, due to her choking on the thermometer, which translated into: 'It's fine,

47

Dad, honest. I just have a bit of a headache.'

Unsurprisingly, Dad didn't believe her. Instead he snapped a dozen photos of her from different angles before posting them on a website he'd set up as a hobby: one for paranoid parents, www.ithinkmychildissuddenlydying.org.

If his daughter had caught some unheard-of tropical illness, then he wanted to know about it. Then he could start panicking properly.

Of course, as you and I know, Kay didn't have a headache at all, but there was no way she was going to tell Dad she'd had a terrifying encounter with a mighty warlock! One whiff of that news and Dad would be marching down Storey Street with a flaming torch!

'I'll be fine, Dad, if I can just have a little rest.' And to back her claim up, she closed her eyes, hoping he would take the hint and give her some space to think.

He didn't, of course.

Instead he sat at the other end of the sofa like a night watchman, just in case the headache freakishly turned into a heart attack, or malaria or something.

Kay might have had her eyes shut, but she knew what he was doing. Knew he'd be sat there, Googling her symptoms for the worst-case scenario. *What if it* is *malaria?* she thought. *Or dengue fever?*

But for some reason, Kay wasn't sharing her dad's fears. Well, not entirely. She'd researched dengue fever only last week and knew her symptoms weren't consistent.

All she could think about was her encounter with the old man.

The mystical way he spoke, his utterances of mountain lions, and the wriggling, writhing sack on his back.

It would have been easier to decide that her wizardly encounter was actually a faint-induced dream, but she knew it wasn't.

The man had spoken to her, and from what he'd said, it sounded like he was a wizard, didn't it? He'd almost threatened to turn her into a mountain lion!

But what did he mean by that? Kay knew she was many things, but a lioness wasn't one of them. She wasn't a cat, or even a kitten. If anything, she was a spineless jellyfish.

Her brain buzzed repeatedly like a faulty doorbell. What could she do to make sense of it all?

She didn't have any friends to confide in, didn't think Fluffy-Poo the otter would give a monkey's, and as for telling Dad? No chance.

He'd probably call the police, or the army, or even the prime minister. More than likely he'd contact all three until the mysterious old man was led away in a straitjacket.

Kay might have been terrified at the prospect of a warlock living down the road, but she was also feeling something else. Something she never ever felt, and something she certainly didn't recognise.

A twitching in her tummy that wasn't nervous cramps. A fluttering in her chest that definitely wasn't anxiety.

She might not have had a clue what she was feeling, dear reader, but I do, and I'm very happy indeed to tell you that what

Kay Catt was feeling was a teeny weeny bit of excitement. And if Kay is extremely eager to know more about this strange old man, then by golly, by gosh, so am I . . . and you'd better be too.

I Dreamed a Dream . . .

Kay Catt dreamed of wizards that night. Of course she did. I mean, wouldn't you?

Eight solid hours of wands, cloaks, incantations, plus a period where she prowled around as a mountain lion – then, weirdly, as a seahorse, but she put that down to the huge chunk of cheese she'd devoured anxiously before bed.

She had no idea what Dad had dreamt about, but judging from his face the next morning, it wasn't pink fluffy clouds or frolicking sheep. His eyes hung so low they looked like they were attached to his face by bungee ropes, and as for the state of his skin? Well, if it was a fancy paint colour, they'd call it 'Shades of Death'.

'I feel . . . unusual,' he moaned, his red nostrils so close to his rice crispies he was in danger of hoovering them up.

'You look . . . awful.' For a second Kay wondered if she really *did* have some incurable illness and had passed it on to her dad.

'You should be in bed.'

'Are you kidding? It's the weekend,' Dad answered. '*Us* time.' And then he sneezed so vigorously that he redecorated the table in the shade 'Bogey Explosion'.

Kay had never seen anything like it, nor did she want to again, and so embarked on the long mission of persuading Dad that:

She would be fine if he went back to bed;

The door was locked so no intruders could abduct her;

If any shape-shifting intruders were able to bypass the locked doors and windows, she would:

i.   SCREAM

ii. PHYSICALLY HURT THEM

iii. CALL DAD IMMEDIATELY

Eventually, and only when he had spray-painted the entire kitchen in 'Spittle Bouquet', did Dad finally crawl back to bed, leaving Kay mighty relieved. Not because she didn't want his vile germs, but because it gave her an opportunity. An opportunity to investigate whether there really was a mighty wizard living on her street.

So with bravery never before seen in a girl of her frail disposition, as soon as Dad was asleep, Kay ventured from the house. Well, she did once she'd triple-checked the cooker was turned off and that all the electrical items were unplugged. (You couldn't be too careful nowadays.)

By the time she got outside, heart walloping in fear, she was lucky Dad hadn't already recovered.

It was a pleasant day out on Storey Street, though. Residents strolled, chatted and washed cars (as was the law at the weekend).

Plenty of kids from Kay's class were out and about too, sitting on the sofa at The House That Was Stolen and playing an elaborate card game that looked more complicated than it was fun.

Kay didn't walk towards them, though, no matter how much she might've wanted to. Her ticker pulsated too wildly to contemplate it for more than a second.

Instead she clutched her wand and walked to the other end of the street. It was as good a place as any to wait for her man of mystery, but it proved ultimately fruitless. He was nowhere to be seen. She meandered up and down the street, jumping whenever a car trundled past and flinching at snails that terrorised her path.

These multitudes of peril soon became too much to bear, as did her inability to find the old man. So, after twenty-two minutes of futile wandering, Kay took the brave step of broadening her search, daring to edge down the ten-foot that separated the crumbly old terraces of Storey Street from the posh semi-detacheds.

What's that, you say? What's a ten-foot? Don't you know anything, dear reader? A ten-foot is a narrow alleyway, called this because they are . . . TEN FEET wide. Get it? Honestly, the youth of today . . .

Anyway, Kay decided to walk down the ten-foot in case it

helped her in her search, despite the humongous perils that lay down there: the cobweb of doom, the empty Coke can of destiny and the slippery dog poo of DEATH!

This was a move of real bravery on her part. She never ventured there on her own, but this flicker of excitement in her was threatening to kick-start into something way, way bigger.

Holding her breath, she forced her way down the alley, past the savage dandelions, until the end was in sight, along with the canal that ran along the back of Storey Street.

Don't get excited, by the way, when you hear the word 'canal'.

Don't imagine for a second that it was reminiscent of the wonderful waterways of Venice. There were no gondolas on this stretch of water, no romantic couples serenading each other from the bridges.

The Storey Street canal was a strange greeny-brown colour: a cocktail of pollution and rust, made worse by endless shopping trollies that had been dumped there since the year 1951.

No one had bothered fishing in it in decades, though one intrepid explorer had tried to canoe down it. He had promptly disappeared, never to be seen again.

Oh, this was a stupid idea, Kay thought to herself. *No self-respecting warlock would bother walking here.* But at the same time, the idea of creeping back down the ten-foot didn't appeal either, not until she'd worked up the necessary bravery, so instead she plodded down the canal, taking in the delights of the half-submerged deckchair and jagged oil barrel. But just as Kay had had enough, something caught her eye. There, some thirty metres ahead, was a shimmering mirage.

What on earth is that? she fretted, the only consolation being that it was some way off and couldn't cut her head off without a very, very long sword.

At this point, Kay would normally turn swiftly and scamper

away. But today was different. Today, for some reason, her brain decided to make her feet start walking forwards, instead of back. Slowly, but forwards all the same.

The horizon edged closer, and so did the shimmering mirage, though it was no longer a purple hue: it now glowed orange, then red, indigo and blue.

Kay's brain prickled with curiosity and recognition. She was still too far away to be sure, but there was every chance she'd found exactly what she was looking for.

Come on in, the Water's ... Lovely

As she crept stealthily along the canal bank, Kay Catt felt like she was in the SAS.

The reality, though, was slightly different. Crack SAS warriors weren't usually so scared that they walked like they needed the world's longest wee. Nor did they whisper, 'What if he turns me into a goat?' under their breath as they hunted their target down.

Twenty metres later, Kay was under no illusion that it was the old man she could see ahead of her, though she had no idea what he was doing.

For some reason, he was bent double over the canal bank, staring deep into the water like it was the world's murkiest crystal ball.

'He's not going to find anything in there, apart from rusted junk and used bog roll,' Kay said to herself, but the old man continued to stare whilst shuffling unsteadily down the bank.

Kay followed, closing the gap still further and noticing that the velvet bag upon his back was moving again, just as it had when she saw him last. It wasn't just the occasional twitch, either. Whatever was trapped inside seemed to be doing the Argentine tango. It didn't bother the old man, though, who trundled along, dipping his long cane into the scuzzy water.

Kay's mind went into overdrive.

What was he doing?

What was in the bag?

Was it something to add to a potion he had bubbling away at home?

Maybe his cauldron was simmering in his kitchen, filled with toads' brains and centipedes' trainers, but he'd realised he had clean run out of eye of newt.

Last time Kay checked, supermarkets didn't stock wizarding necessities apart from at Halloween, which would explain the trip to the canal.

Her tortured head could just about cope with this idea, but then another thought flashed into her mind.

Unless someone had poured radioactive waste into the canal and transformed the newts into mutant ones, then she was barking up the wrong tree. The thing struggling in the bag was way bigger, and so irate that it seemed to be wearing boxing gloves. It couldn't be a . . . a child, could it?

This was enough to tip Kay over the edge. All of a sudden, she believed she'd been lured into a trap.

The old man was a wizard, and not a smiley one like Dumblewotsit out of *You-Know-What*. He was a dark and sinister overlord like Saru-thingy out of *Lord of the Bing-Bongs* (I never did read fantasy books properly).

What if he had descended on Storey Street because he'd already kidnapped every child where he *used* to live, and, having boiled their bones to increase his devilish powers, was now looking for fresh Seacross meat?

Kay could see it now. He might look old and doddery, but he'd lured her here on purpose. All it would take was one muttered spell and a wave of his staff and she would be powerless to his every whim.

He'd stuff her in the sack and smuggle her home. Within minutes she'd be dangling by her sock over his cauldron, and if she was brave enough she'd look down to see the tortured faces of other unfortunate children, as well as the newt eyes, bat wings and toad armpit hair. The potion would be bubbling like a devilishly hot curry, and when he dipped her into it?

Well, it would jolly well hurt!

The thought of excruciating pain was too much for Kay to bear. Fearing for her life, she turned to run, but in her haste tripped over a bent bicycle wheel left on the bank. With a pained wail, she flew face first, screaming loudly enough to wake not only the dead but the entire population of Australia. Not surprisingly, she also caught the attention of the old man, who turned his attention away from the canal, lifting his cane from the water in the process.

'Good lord,' he said, stunned. 'What are you doing down there, my dear old thing?'

Kay wasn't listening. She was so petrified she was only able to use one of her senses at a time, and her eyes were currently in operation, glaring bulbously at the end of the old man's staff.

You see, it wasn't a normal old walking stick any more, oh no. The wizard had transformed it into something wicked, something dastardly.

There, on the end, was a large rusty hook. A hook that Kay *knew* was destined for her. It would catch her and deposit her straight into the old man's sack.

'D-d-don't hurt me,' she wailed as she scrambled backwards.

'You w-w-wouldn't, would you? 'Cos don't forget, I'm a m-m-mountain l—'

But she never got to finish her sentence, as the bank ran out beneath her feet, sending her toppling backwards into the putrid canal.

The stench hit her like an intercity train, an indescribable mulch of decay and hideousness that raced up her nostrils as she was sucked head first beneath the water.

She tried to fight – of course she did – but her thrashing left arm caught on a discarded pram, wedged solid in the mud. No matter how hard she wriggled, she couldn't free her sleeve, and as the oxygen in her body decreased, so did her resolve.

Helplessly, she looked skywards, squinting through the goo, and the last thing she saw as her eyes closed was a hook piercing the water, coming mercilessly to claim her.

What a way to go, thought Kay. *What a way to g—*

Hubble, Bubble, Kay's in Trouble

Waking up was a surprise to Kay. In those last moments of turmoil, she'd taken the tiniest solace in the belief that the wizard would kill her before dunking her into his cauldron like an enormous digestive biscuit.

So to find her eyes flickering open and her lungs working (once she'd spat up a lungful of frogspawn) was a delightful surprise. Or it was, until she realised that this meant the wizard planned to sacrifice her while she was still alive.

'Ah,' she said, although her captor was not as smart or as thorough as he might have been. For starters, he hadn't gagged her, or swollen her tongue to the size of a surfboard to stop her yelling for help. Quite an oversight, I'm sure you'd agree.

But as much as she wanted to, Kay didn't cry out for help. Not knowing where she was, or even if she was still living in the same realm, there seemed no point in yelling.

...maybe the old man had dragged her though a portal that he kept in the back of his wardrobe or his washing machine, to a place where winged buffalo roamed the skies and the sun was made out of strawberry blancmange.

Don't judge Kay by the quality of these imaginings. The poor love was feeling pretty darned stressed.

The other thing that troubled her, apart from being kidnapped by an all-powerful sorcerer, was the fact that he hadn't bothered to tie her up either. No ropes, tape or even shackles fashioned from unicorn hair, the most powerful substance known to man (. . . apart from Pritt Stick).

It was almost as if the old man didn't want to keep her captive. And despite the overwhelming sense of *Oh my lord, I'm doomed* racing round her skull, Kay wasn't going to lie there and wait for him to sheep-dip her into his cauldron.

Instead, she allowed her eyes to acclimatise, and after thirty seconds she could make out the shadowiest corners of her cell. Well, I say a cell – turns out it was more of a dining room, though not a very well decorated one. The walls were grey and cobwebby. *Hardly surprising for a sinister wizard*, thought Kay.

There was nothing on the walls, and there weren't even any curtains hanging at the window – only a drab blanket that had been tacked to the frame. As for the rest of the décor? Well, there wasn't any – just a single coffee table and a succession of boxes, with contents occasionally spilling out, like tweed cloaks and elaborate silky waistcoats. For some reason, Kay felt compelled to look in them, though she had no idea why. *Concentrate on escaping*, she demanded of herself, *not on the state of his wardrobe*.

Silently, she made for the door, but only managed to trip over a box and smack into the coffee table, disturbing a silver photo frame.

'No!' Kay gasped. If the frame smashed, it'd echo round the whole house. No way she'd escape with that kind of commotion. With a dexterity that she didn't know she possessed, Kay threw herself towards the falling frame and caught it just as it kissed the floorboards.

'Oh my goodness, oh my word,' she said, clutching the frame to her chest as if it contained a photo of someone precious to her.

Once her breathing settled, she allowed herself to look at the frame, eyes widening as she saw the image that nestled inside. It was him, the wizard, but not as she knew him: he looked younger, less wizened. There were fewer lines on his face and his hair was shorter, neater, and so was his beard. Instead of a cloak, he was draped in a suit, and his smile was so bright it glinted. It really didn't look like him. 'Must've been his day off,' Kay said to herself. 'Maybe even wizards have weekends.'

He wasn't alone in the photo either, as beside him was a woman. The same age, maybe slightly older, with the same long, white hair that now grew from his head. It was so long it made Rapunzel's 'do look like a crew cut.

Kay stared at the woman, and the woman stared right back. There was a kindness to her, but also a sadness, like she could see something terrible coming over the photographer's shoulder.

Kay felt sorry for her, but then shook the thought from her head. They looked so happy together that she must be a witch too. An evil, dark, brooding sorceress with the same hideous intentions as him!

And if that was the case, then she didn't deserve her sympathy. Taking care not to make a sound, Kay put the frame back in its place and tiptoed towards the door.

The hallway wasn't as dark as the dining room, though it was twice as dusty, and as Kay made her way, she realized that this house was the mirror image of her own. They were so identical that she expected to look up the stairs and see the photo of Dad, Mum and herself hanging there.

Curiosity eating at her, she peered up to the landing, but there was no picture.

There was just a cobweb, which pulled her back to reality. She might be in a tatty old house on Storey Street, but she still needed to get out of it, sharpish. So she tiptoed towards the front door, just as a repetitive thud started pounding from inside the living room.

'What's that?' she whispered, before adding, 'And why am I even intrigued when I'm so darned scared?'

But the truth was, as much as she didn't want to admit it, this whole incident had got under her skin. This wasn't her normal kind of fear for once. She wanted to run for the hills, of course she did. But it was different too. The fear was mixed with a weird curiosity that seemed to add glue to the soles of her trainers, which was really odd for a Scaredy Catt like her.

And so, before her cowardice kicked back in, Kay Catt edged closer and closer to the living room door, and the rhythmic pounding that lay beyond it . . .

10

Big Fish, Small Fish, Cardboard boxes

With a deep breath, Kay edged the living room door open.

Just a touch, enough to let her peek inside without being seen. What she was hoping or expecting to find, she had no idea. All she knew was that she couldn't leave the house without understanding what was going on.

Sometimes, though, the act of seeing something doesn't do you any good. It doesn't make things any clearer. And this was the case here, as Kay was met with the oddest of sights.

Scattered around the room was a huge array of cardboard boxes: some small, some large, but every single one of them looked full to the brim, with random objects spilling from the tops.

In the middle of the room stood the old man, without his cloak, but still wearing his broken cone hat. He was also sporting a velvet waistcoat, kaleidoscopic in colour.

In his left hand he clutched his staff, and Kay sighed in relief to see the hook had disappeared. It had a new purpose now, as the wizard waved it extravagantly in the air like a conductor's baton, to accompany the heavy bass beats that Kay had heard through the walls.

It was a deeply odd image. Who'd have thought that ancient wizards could possibly love dance music? And not just any dance music, either. This was the kind so heavy in bass that it shook the money from your piggy bank and the fillings from your teeth.

Kay could feel the walls vibrate as the music got both louder and faster, and saw the old man's grin stretch so wide you'd need half a dozen toothbrushes to keep his gnashers clean.

His arms waved wildly, circling like a helicopter's propellers, but just as he looked set to hover above the ground, he flicked his stick in the direction of the far wall and the most bizarre thing happened. Out of nowhere came a piercing shaft of blue light.

'AAAARRRGGHHHH!' squealed Kay, fearing the wizard had just opened a portal into an uncharted, parallel realm. Her shout wasn't quiet but no one heard her – the music made sure of that, even when she screamed again and again as the light began to bounce and strobe, splitting into two beams, then three, four, five and six.

Within thirty seconds, dozens of lights fizzed against the walls, dancing and pulsing, throwing beams upon the ecstatic face of the old man as he conducted wildly. Kay's eyes were like saucers now, too scared to blink.

Instead, she stood and stared as the music hit yet another peak. But just as the scene couldn't get any weirder, it did. The old man stopped spinning his arms and started beckoning to all four corners of the room, whilst making kissing motions with his lips.

'What is he doing?!' Kay whispered to herself. Tempting a legion of goblins from the shadows? Brainwashed, obedient minions to do his dirty kidnapping work for him?

She didn't have a clue, but she was so scared she forced her legs to back away. But as she turned, Kay saw something emerge from the shadows. Not a goblin, nor a gremlin, nor a unicorn or dragon. It was a . . . kitten. A thin, undernourished excuse for a kitten, but a kitten all the same.

'What the . . . ?' said Kay. 'What does he want with a defenceless kitten?'

Now, this in itself wasn't a completely random sight. Witches and wizards are well known for their feline friends, though lord knows why. I mean, cats are rubbish, aren't they?

They don't fetch sticks if you throw them, and they bury their own poos, unlike dogs, who have wonderful senses of humour and leave their droppings for people to slip on in a comedy manner.

Anyway. I digress. What made this sight unusual was that we weren't talking about one cat here. Not two, three, four or seventeen. We were talking about dozens. A hundred, possibly.

From every corner, every nook, every cardboard box they came, each of them meowing in delight as their master called them out.

Within seconds, they were gathering at Kay's feet, rubbing against her sodden trouser legs. Seconds later, they were shinning their way rhythmically up to her knees. Within a minute, it was like she wearing her own life-size cat cardigan. A cardigan she neither liked nor wanted.

Is this how she was destined to die? Suffocated by a living, breathing sea of kittens?

This left Kay with no other option but to writhe and buck like a rodeo bull who's discovered they're carrying a killer shark instead of a cowboy.

But no matter how rigorously she shook, the kittens held on.

In fact, more of them jumped on board, forcing her to the floor
as a few last, pleading words fell from her lips.

'Don't hurt me!' she wailed, desperate to catch the wizard's
eye, desperate for him to call off his evil, merciless plan. 'Please
don't kill me. I have so much to live foooooooooor . . .'

Dream a Little Dream of Me

'Hurt you?' came a voice.

It was muffled through the carpet of cats covering Kay's entire body, not to mention the music, but still loud enough to hear.

'Kill you? Why, you silly sausage. The chances of my friends or me hurting you are zero, zilch, nada. These friends of mine aren't killers, they are dancers!'

Kay saw the old man smile before smashing his staff down into the floor with almighty, ear-splitting thwack.

The effect was instantaneous.

The cats sped from Kay's body to the centre of the living room floor, and there, under the spell of the Storey Street Sorcerer, they started to . . . dance.

Yep, you heard right. These cats started dancing. Spinning tails, shimmying on their hind legs. Kay swore she saw one cheeky feline attempt a cartwheel.

On hind legs.

Now, none of them were exactly ballroom dancers: they weren't sporting sequins or a spray tan, but they were definitely entranced by both the music and the mesmeric laser show that bounced from wall to wall.

And there was no doubt that the old man was the puppet-master at the middle of it all.

Kay had never seen anything like it. And she'd seen her dad do some random things, like encasing a staple gun in bubble wrap and blunting the point on the protractor that lived in her pencil case.

It didn't matter how many times she blinked in disbelief; as soon as her eyes were open, there was another moshing moggie, and another and another.

It was the most bonkers flash mob she'd ever seen in her life.

There they stood, on two feet, pawing at the strobing lights, whilst others chased their tails until they fell over drunk. Some were shimmying up the trouser leg of the wizard until it looked like he was wearing a cloak of tabby tweed.

There they swung, meowing happily as their master weaved his dastardly spell.

'How are you doing that?' she yelled over the music.

'Sorry?' he replied, cupping a hand to his ear.

'I said, how are you doing that? You must be a w-w-w—'

'That's right!' the old man hollered ecstatically, as if Kay had just explained the process of making diamonds out of bogeys. 'I am indeed a "W". "W" for Wilf. How incredibly perceptive!'

'No, not that! You're a w-w-w—'

'That is also true. Wilkinson is my last name, though I shan't be telling you my middle name. A man has to maintain some air of mystery, you know.'

On his conducting went.

'Well, I know your game. I know who you really are. I know that you're a . . . WIZARD!'

At the sound of that word, Wilf Wilkinson finally stopped, and with a wave of his staff, turned the volume down a tad. 'Oh, *that!*' he chortled. 'Well I suppose, looking at me, there's no denying that!'

He sat slowly and stiffly on a tatty armchair and pondered out loud as he plaited his beard.

'Wizards are old men – check. Wizards are wise, noble and often eccentric – check. Beard – check. Outlandish clothes – check. Rather fetching hat – check!'

Kay joined in, super excitedly. It was true. It was *true!*

'Powerful enough to make an army of kittens dance – checkity check!'

Wilf blushed and tried to interrupt, but Kay hadn't finished.

'All-powerful warlock with the ability to turn girls into mountain lions – checkity-checkity-che—'

'Now, now, my dear old thing.' He blushed. 'I merely observed the immense potential that you very clearly hold.'

'So are you, then?' she asked. 'Are you a wizard . . . or not?'

Wilf pondered this awhile, twirling his beard like a cowboy's lasso. 'Do you know? I'm not sure that's for me to decide. Maybe I should let you make up your own mind, hmm? After all, you've seen me in action, haven't you?'

With that, he waved his arms dramatically once more, prompting the music to blare louder.

'My Wilma always told me that we can be whoever we wanted to be. Tell me, my child, do you think me magical?'

Kay was under no illusion about that one.

'I saw you, down by the canal, and your staff had a magical hook on it. You were looking for something, probably to cook in a cauldron. There were things wriggling in your sack too. They were alive, you can't deny it.'

'And why would I, my anxious little firebrand? Yes, I have a hook, and I suppose it is rather magical. After all, if I didn't have it I'd simply fall into the canal, and that would never do. How would I rescue some of my friends then?'

He picked up a particularly scraggy kitten, who batted at his beard like it was a ball of wool. 'Breaks my heart to see people treat such wonderful, kind creatures in such a barbarous way.'

'The cats? You were looking for cats . . . in a canal?' Kay stared at the wee thing, looking for hidden gills and scales.

Wilf nodded sadly. 'Can you believe people could be so cruel? Why get a cat in the first place if you don't have the space or the heart to look after it? What sort of troll would' – the old man paused and wrapped his hands round the kitten's ears – 'dump the poor thing in the canal with a brick tied round its collar?'

'Does that really happen?'

'It does. Not always, but still too often. I walk the length of the canal most weeks – well, as far as my legs will carry me, anyway. It was something we always did togethe—'

'We?' interrupted Kay.

Wilf looked flustered before changing the subject sadly. 'You'd be amazed how many of the poor things I find dumped in there . . . some of them beyond my help – not that I give up until I've used every bit of magic at my disposal.'

'So what are you going to do with them?' Kay looked around for the cauldron that she felt MUST exist. 'Why save them if all you're going to do next is boil them?'

The old man let loose with a shriek so piercing he was in danger of summoning the entire dog population of Seacross. He shuffled round the room, trying to console every cat he could lay a hand on. 'There, there, my beauty. Take no notice of the girl; she's clearly concussed, or just plain BATTY!'

Kay recoiled. 'Me, batty? Scared, maybe, but not batty. I-I-I mean, you look like Dumbledore, you don't deny you're a wizard . . . and well, forgive me for saying this, but wizards do have cauldrons, don't they?'

The old man looked slightly calmer, pleased perhaps to have been compared to such a legendary warlock. 'That's very kind, my dear, but isn't it witches who have cauldrons? I've only got this.'

He pointed to a grubby microwave oven that looked like it had twelve-year-old porridge welded to it. 'I only use it to warm their milk up in. Can't remember when I cooked anything in it for me.'

Kay had watched every film about wizards ever made, and she'd never seen a potion concocted in such a machine, even if they were in a hurry. So she scanned the room, looking for anything even vaguely bowl-like, but apart from a dirty breakfast bowl, there was nothing.

Maybe Wilf *didn't* eat. Maybe he couldn't afford it. Must cost a fortune to feed all those hungry moggy mouths.

What there was, though, was a clock on a mantelpiece, which shook Kay back into reality.

'2.30?' she squealed. 'It can't be. Feels like I left home half an hour ago. My dad's going to go mental!' She pulled a soggy, lifeless mobile phone from her pocket.

'If he's woken up he'll have called the police. The army. The SAS. He'll hire Sherlock Holmes and a pack of bloodhounds to track me down.'

Wilf smiled. 'Well, he sounds like a hoot! Don't worry, you can tell him you're always safe with Wilf. Anything even comes near you and pif-paf-poof!' He chuckled and waved his staff in her direction, accidentally making the music still louder.

'I've got to go, Wilf . . . er . . . thanks. Thanks for everything!'

The old man looked crestfallen.

'You will come back, won't you? See me again? My friends here, they're clearly very drawn to you.'

How on earth did Kay answer that? Her head screamed *NO WAY, YOU'RE A LUNATIC!* whereas her heart, well, it yelled something else completely.

'Er . . . possibly,' she said to herself as she ran. 'Tomorrow maybe. Or the day after. Or neither. Or both!'

And on she sprinted, sporting both a smile and a frown simultaneously.

Don't Panic...!

Kay expected to leave the bonkers world firmly behind her in Wilf's house, but as she tore through his front gate at the far end of Storey Street, it seemed like the old man had infected other people too.

Pelting down the pavement, she couldn't help but notice the chaos going on behind a number of front doors. She heard screams and bangs and howls. She even saw Rick Dee from number 59 standing on his dining table, bashing at the floor with a broken broom handle. What was going on was beyond her, and she had worries of her own to deal with, especially when she spotted a police car idling in front of her house.

'Oh no,' she gasped. 'No, no, no, no, NO!' This could only mean one thing. That Dad had woken up, found the house empty, and gone bat-brained mental.

Kay tried to think of an excuse that didn't sound like she'd traded brains with a dung beetle. But how could you explain what had just happened to her, without a phone call being made to burly men carrying straitjackets?

It wasn't a question she had time to answer, as the front door flew open and whirlwind Dad whipped her up into his arms.

'Kay!' he yelled snottily, a yucky mixture of flu and raw emotion. 'Where have you been??'

'Er . . . out?'

Obvious, but not a lie.

'I thought you'd been kidnapped,' Dad wept. 'I thought you'd been snatched by bandits.'

'Da-ad,' Kay moaned, as he snotted and sneezed into her lughole. She wasn't sure what was worse, his mucus or his mithering.

From behind Dad appeared Police Chief Waggle, who seemed more interested in the digestive he was dunking in his tea than her blessed reappearance.

'Oh, you're home,' he mumbled through a mouthful of crumbs. 'And I've just sent the sergeant out for more Hobnobs. Still, there's the rest of the shift to go. They won't go to waste.' Draining his cuppa in one gulp, he left, but not before he warned Kay about scaring her dad again.

He also dipped his hand into the biscuit tin one last time. Just for old times' sake.

Dad watched as Waggle drove away, a stack of digestives in his mouth, before turning back to his daughter. His face was no longer relieved, but thunderous.

'Where have you been? Why did you scare me? And why were you gone so long? Have you any idea how it felt to wake up and find you missing?'

'I'm sorry, Dad, I'm sorry, it's just . . . I was . . .'

What was the right word to say next? 'Bored'? 'Lonely'? 'Intrigued by a wizard that's moved in up the road?' None of those answers were going to wash with Dad, that was for sure.

'Well? I'm waiting?'

'It's a secret.' Again, not strictly a lie.

'What sort of answer is that?' 'The truth?'

'Well on this occasion the truth isn't good enough. Not when it worried me sick.'

'Would you rather I lied, then?'

'I'd rather you didn't leave the house on a whim. I'd rather you told me exactly what happened! It's a dangerous, cruel place out there, Kay, and it's my job to look after you. Just like I should've looked after Mum.'

Well, that was it. The mere mention of Mum's death prompted the truth to tumble out like an acrobat during their encore.

'I fell in the canal,' she gabbled. 'I fell in the canal, and an old man fished me out with his staff. His magical staff. Then he carried me home and introduced me to his cats, who he entranced before making them dance to drum and bass.'

Dad looked mortified. Mortified and angry.

'Kay Catt. This is your last chance. The truth.'

'This is the truth. The truth is, I think there's a wizard living on our street. A proper, magic-making, wand-wielding wizard. Now that's just about the most terrifying thing I've ever thought about, but at the same time, it might be the most exciting. I mean, imagine, Dad. Imagine that!'

She'd had no idea she was going to say that. All she did know was that her dad stood in front of her, nose streaming and head shaking.

'Kay Catt. I can't even begin to tell you how disappointed I am. Not just that you would worry me sick on purpose by disappearing like that. But that you'd then lie to me about it too. I mean, wizards! Here. On our street. The very thought of it.'

'But Dad—'

But Dad wasn't listening. Not a chance.

'Because if there was a wizard living amongst us, do you think I'd ever let you out of the house again? HHHM? Now, I'd suggest you go to your room, and you stay there until you realise just how ridiculous you sound. Do you understand me?'

It wasn't a question Kay could answer. She didn't understand anything about what was happening to her. So, obediently as always, she did what her dear old dad told her, despite every step feeling like a mile.

Silence is Golden (Plated)

Waiting is rubbish. It doesn't matter if it's for a bus, a dentist, or for a shower of golden coins to rain down upon your lap, it's the waiting bit that gets on your nerves.

So it was for young Kay Catt, who spent the rest of the afternoon waiting for a knock at her bedroom door and the inevitable health and safety discussion from her dad.

But the weird thing was, it didn't come. There was no knock. There was no lecture. Not a single pie chart or Venn diagram was shoved under her nose to highlight the increased risk of accidental death by lying about hanging out with wizards.

This could mean only one of two things: that there *were* no statistics to back up Dad's fears, or the shock of Kay's revelation had killed him quicker than an athlete with leopard's legs running the hundred metres.

Kay was a worrier – it was impossible not to be with a dad like hers – but she reckoned it had to be a lack of proof rather than sudden death that had kept Dad from her door. But two and a half hours in, her imagination started to get the better of her.

What if her going missing *had* shoved Dad through death's door? What if, all these years, he'd been carrying a rare, unidentified heart condition that could only be triggered by the actions of a cruel, wayward but well-meaning daughter?

If his heart had exploded, then it felt like hers would too. But if hers didn't explode, then what would become of her? She'd be on her own. Left to grow up on Seacross's mean streets. Or maybe she'd just get dumped in the canal like one of Wilf's kittens? Either way, she didn't like the sound of it. And so, cracking her knuckles in readiness to perform heart massage, she dashed towards his bedroom.

But Dad's heart hadn't exploded. Course it hadn't. Because I'm telling this story, and to be honest I'm a bit squeamish about stuff like that. I boil an egg for three days before eating it, because runny yolk makes my belly go funny.

Dad was alive, but ill. Kay found him in bed, tangled in his sheets as he thrashed beneath the weight of his fever.

It was scary. Not as scary as finding your dad's bedroom walls decorated in a new shade called 'Heart Explosion', but scary enough.

He was moaning and wailing in his sleep, and from what Kay could gather, he was dreaming about her. It was hard to understand, but from what she could gather, she was in constant danger, firstly from drowning in a vat of trifle, then from being stabbed to death by a runaway pincushion, then finally, and most disturbingly, by being sucked into a vacuum cleaner and suffocated into an early grave.

It wasn't exactly the way she wanted to spend her afternoon, but she couldn't help but feel responsible, and so eased her guilt by patting his fevered brow with a damp cloth, just like he did in her illest moments.

Minutes became hours, hours became the whole night. Sunday morning became Sunday afternoon . . . You get the message, don't you? Dad was really rather poorly.

And do you know what? Lovely Kay didn't panic about it. Well, she did a bit, but not in a OH MY GOODNESS CALL AN AMBULANCE!!! kind of way.

Instead, she recognised it was a fever – a nasty one at that – and did everything she could to keep Dad calm, cool and hydrated.

It was often difficult work.

Dad was doing odd things. He didn't recognise her, and he'd

swear and wail at the walls. He'd get so thirsty she'd find him in the bathroom, drinking out of the toilet bowl.

He seemed to be enjoying it so much Kay wondered whether to add a segment of lemon and a straw, but fetched instead a large bottle of clean water. It had to be better than the stuff with Domestos and soggy loo roll in it.

While Dad drank the equivalent of the Atlantic Ocean, Kay changed his drenched sheets. Then she helped him back to bed, while he dribbled and moaned and mistook her for his Great Aunt Petunia, who had apparently accused him of stealing the last biscuit from the tin in 1982. Kay had no idea who Aunt Petunia was, but boy, did her dad HATE her.

There were calmer moments too. And in those times she read (about wizards, obviously) and watched films (about wizards, obviously). And do you know what? She was calm. And almost content.

By the time dawn on Monday arrived, Kay had more experience than many battlefield nurses, but still Dad's fever hadn't broken, though his sleep was less trifley.

Content that he could be left to sleep without choking on his own tortured dreams, Kay readied herself for school, simultaneously hopeful and fearful that she might bump into Wilf on the way.

So, after forcing herself to eat breakfast, picking up her wand and checking that she didn't still smell of the canal, she set off for school.

I'd like to be able to tell you that it was calmer out on Storey Street than it was in Kay's head, but that would be a fat old granny of a lie. It was anything but. It was a wind tunnel of trouble and strife. Just like yesterday afternoon, there seemed to be various commotions breaking out, but in a lot more houses. There were screams and stampedes and hissy-fits. Everywhere she looked, Kay saw people dashing about with brooms and hockey sticks and cricket bats, thrashing at the floor like they were under attack.

Maybe, Kay worried, *Wilf had something to do with it? Maybe his shadowy plans were taking effect?*

Just as the racket was sucking up the remainder of Kay's attention, her ears were invaded by laughter, instead of screams, on the other side of the street. And it didn't take her long to realize who was at the heart of it: those lumbering lumpheads, Saliva Shreeve and Bunions Bootle.

Now, this pair weren't known for their intellect. In fact, they thought intellect was a town in Belgium, not a measure of their brain capacity. What they *were* famous for was mental and physical torture – or bullying, as it was more commonly known. And Kay knew instantly who they were after today.

There he was, poor old Wilf, forcing his creaky legs into action, only to have his every step interrupted by homemade firecrackers thrown beneath his feet. Wilf looked dumbfounded by the bombs exploding beneath his cloak, and kept staring at his staff, presumably wondering if his magic was being especially powerful today. Perhaps he'd eaten one too many shredded wheat for breakfast?

He lifted his stick and shook it vigorously, expecting to summon more sparks from it, but when none came it caused him to become more and more confused and wave the stick more and more wildly.

His tormentors, of course, found this utterly hilarious, yelping and clapping like a pair of seals drunk on wine gums.

Others, the likes of Jake Biggs, Michael J Mouse and Liv and Daisy Smith, followed them, all of them telling the bullies to leave the man alone, and all of them being roundly and completely ignored.

Kay couldn't help but admire them: how she wished she had the bravery to stand up for her friend. But the mere thought of it made her feel more unsteady than a bridge made out of soggy crisps.

All she could do was follow in their wake and tremble.

With every step she took she tried to summon up her mountain lion, but her roars were nothing more than an apology.

She was helpless, hopeless, and if she didn't find her bravery super quick, then her new pal Wilf was in a whole lot of bother.

Eye of the (Mountain) Tiger

Poor old Wilf. He might have been madder than an Arctic explorer dressed in a bikini, but he still didn't realise what was going on around him.

Because he was a big-hearted man, he thought the attention of Saliva and Bunions was a positive thing: that they were laughing *with* him, rather than *at* him. Kay could see that he was bemused by the whole firecracker thing as well, couldn't work out why his mystical cloak seemed to be banging and smouldering every few seconds.

'Come on, Wilf,' Kay fretted. 'Do something about it. Turn them into something embarrassing, make their heads explode – do something, PLEASE!'

But all the old man did was hobble on, grinning at the attention and trying to engage the pair in conversation.

'Wonderful day!' he sang. 'A triumph! Enough to make your

soul sing!'

But his pleasantries served only as fuel to their ever-growing fires, as they mimicked him cruelly, repeating his every word in grotesque parrot fashion.

Kay reached the back of the crowd and saw Wilf nearing a crossroads. In front of him were two signs, pointing in opposite directions, and both of them read, 'Warning. Humiliation ahead.'

'Ohmylordohmylordohmylord,' she mouthed. She wanted to run – home, away, anywhere she wouldn't witness the disaster ahead. But at the same time, she wanted to help, to step in, to put those wallies in their place. But how could she? Where would she find the bravery?

She gripped hard at her wand, brandishing it in their direction, but it felt as useless as a toothpick in the hands of a caveman who had a large piece of tyrannosaurus rex stuck between his teeth.

Fortunately for Wilf, the other kids were feeling a little bit braver.

'Stop!' Michael Mouse yelled, hands on hips like the wannabe superhero he was.

'That's . . . enough!' shouted Daisy and Liv, reading each others minds.

The bullies didn't listen. They never do, do they? They just laughed and poured scorn on them from a great height.

'Oooooh, listen to these do-gooders!' they laughed. 'Oh, on second thoughts . . . don't. LOSERS!'

Kay felt her insides tremble like an underset jelly. What could she do? What could she possibly say? And why, for that matter, wasn't Wilf helping himself either?

Up ahead, the old man suddenly looked startled as a small blue flame flickered from a thread on the hem of his cloak. Within seconds, the flicker was a dance, then a tango, then a samba, until the flame stomped dangerously up towards his calves.

'Oh my!' he gasped, beating at his legs with his staff and blowing like an asthmatic big bad wolf. 'Oh goodness. Oh dear!'

Suddenly the bully boys weren't quite so bullish.

'What do we do?' screamed Bunions.

'It wasn't us?' shrieked Saliva.

'Water!' replied Jake Biggs, which had dozens of kids reaching into their lunch boxes and pulling out flasks and cartons of juice. Feverishly, straws were inserted and lids unscrewed until a sugary torrent flew in Wilf's direction, soaking him, but with insufficient power to douse the flames.

Kay panicked. Course she did. So did Bunions and Saliva, who legged it in opposite directions, as did a lot of the others in the crowd. Only a select few bravehearts remained.

'Wilf!' Kay yelled. 'Take off the cloak!' She wanted to run to him, to stamp on the flames herself, but frankly she didn't dare.

The old man did his best: his gnarly fingers fumbled at the bow, managing to pull the knot into a tangled spaghetti mess that would bamboozle a scout leader.

Think, Kay, THINK! she thought. She couldn't call the fire brigade as her phone was still waterlogged, and besides, her fingers had turned blue with fear.

She should've told someone else to call, but every time she

opened her mouth, nothing came out but stale, fearful air.

And time was running out. The flames were getting bigger.

'We've got to do something, and quick!' yelled Mouse
(he'd heard it in a Batman movie once), and fortunately for him,
the Smith twins were already on it, dashing through the nearest
front gate.

'Look . . .' yelled Daisy.

'. . . A hose!' shouted Liv.

They were right. There it was, tethered to the wall.

With nimble fingers, they pulled it from it from its mooring
and dashed back in the direction of the old man.

'Kay!' Daisy yelled. 'Turn . . .'

'. . . the tap on!' added Liv.

Now, this was something Kay could do, as it meant she was
running *away* from the trouble rather than *towards* it.

On rubbery legs, she dashed to the tap and turned it, just as
the twins reached Wilf.

But – disastrous disaster. Nothing happened! No water. Not a
spurt, not a trickle, not a drop.

'WAAAAAAAAHHHH!' wailed Wilf from the other side of the
hedge. The flames were licking higher and more angrily, heading
north of his knees.

'Ohmylordohmylordohmylord,' replied Kay.

Hands shaking, she pulled the hose end from the tap, but this served only to soak her trainers as water poured upon them. If the tap had water in it, then why, oh why, wasn't the stupid hose working??

'Kay?' yelled Daisy in the distance. 'What's going . . .'

'. . . on?' finished Liv. 'Turn on the blooming tap!!'

Kay rammed the hose back over the tap. 'Working now?'

There was a pause. A heart-splitting, nerve-shredding beat.

'*NO!!*' came the reply.

Kay's ticker was on the verge of combustion. She couldn't do this, she couldn't do this, she couldn't do this. But just as she convinced herself that she couldn't do this, guess what, she realised that maybe she could. Because she noticed, by the front gate, a kink in the hose. The sort of kink that would stop water passing through.

With the speed of an eight-legged cheetah, she sprinted towards it – only to trip over a gnome that was fishing on the lawn when there clearly wasn't a drop of water in sight.

Fearing she didn't even have time to stand up again, Kay crawled like a baby who'd just drunk a gallon of high-energy milk, until she fell upon the hose and wrestled it straight.

Whooooosh! The water powered onwards, making the hose dance and writhe as it passed through the gate.

Kay listened intently for clues on the other side of the hedge, weeping in relief when Wilf's cries of 'Hot hot hot!!' morphed into 'Cold cold cold!!'

She knew then that the water had reached him, and as she dashed back on to Storey Street, she prayed no serious damage had been done.

It bloomin' hadn't either, as Wilf felt the temperature in his nether regions drop from an Amazonian 50 degrees to 40, to 30, to 20, until only seconds later, it felt like he was holidaying in Grimsby in January.

'I think you can turn the tap off now, my dear old thing,' gargled Wilf. 'I showered last week so I don't have shampoo with me!'

Kay giggled. She had no idea how he managed to joke when he'd almost become a kebab.

'I don't know how to thank you,' Wilf said, eyes glistening with something other than hose water.

'It was the twins' idea,' Kay said, meaning it entirely. 'I froze, didn't I? Did nothing, as usual.'

That's not . . . true,' added the twins. 'We spotted the hose, but without water . . . well, it's a bit useless, isn't it?'

'Very true, very true!' Wilf beamed at a blushing Kay. 'You are all heroes. Without you I would've been toast! You must let me return the favour and escort you safely to school?'

'We'll be OK,' answered the twins. 'It's only over the road.'

But Kay was delighted to spend even the briefest of times with her new pal. 'Yes,' she said, 'that would be magical.'

And with their heads held high and chests puffed out, the unlikely pair made their way on towards school.

School's Out

Kay felt . . . different throughout school that morning. A bit taller, a bit broader, a bit braver.

Double Maths was always boring, but it was doubly dull after the earlier exploits. And when Kay thought of her part in saving Wilf, she felt, well, a little bit proud.

Just to put a whopping great cherry on the cake/situation, Saliva and Bunions didn't get away with their misdemeanors, either. They were hauled in front of the headmaster, Mr Peach, and made to empty their bags, which contained the following:

4 mouldy conkers

2kg of home-made firecrackers

A penny dating back to 1941

A brick

A hand grenade (minus pin)

A hand grenade pin

A curious fungus (which may or may not be the cure to all known illnesses)

They were then packed off home, much to Kay's delight.

It couldn't get any better, it really couldn't. Until, of course, it did.

How, I hear you cry? How could Wilf's tormentors getting their deserved comeuppance possibly be improved on?

Well, if you'll give me a minute, I'll tell you.

Just as the playtime bell was about to toll, in panted a puffed-out student called Dennis Gee, who shoved a note into Miss Maybury's hands.

'Mr Peach says you're to read this out immediately,' he gasped. 'And that you shouldn't panic!' He turned to the other kids before shouting, 'Don't panic!!' He looked like he rather needed to hear his own advice.

Miss Maybury looked at the boy quizzically before reading the note and turning a ghostly shade of terrified.

'Class. There has been a change of plan. You are all to return home immediately. School will be closed for the rest of the day.'

Faces lit up like light bulbs (an obvious image, I know, but effective). Huzzahs and hurrahs bounced off the walls. Everyone was delighted, except for the class swot, Finley McGinley, who asked the question no one else was bothered about.

'But why, Miss? Why?'

Miss Maybury fixed him with a queasy expression, before looking uneasily under the desk.

'Vermin, Finley. Vermin. Mice have been spotted in the school kitchen. And not just one of them, either. A platoon, a legion, an army of the beasts, hell bent on eating our Arctic rolls, before moving on to us for pudding.'

Finley (ever the swot) tried to point out to Miss M that Arctic rolls were *actually* a pudding, but she strangely wasn't interested. Instead, she tucked her trousers into her socks and picked up a cricket bat from the store room, before leading the children out to the school gates.

It was a strange atmosphere out there, a mixture of jubilation and terror, as people started to learn that the mice weren't just troubling the school kitchen, but many of the houses up and down the street.

It all started to make sense to Kay now: the strange behaviour she'd seen through windows, the horror etched on her neighbours' faces.

It should've made her terrified. It should've made her shake in her boots. But do you know what? *It didn't.* Well, not as much as usual. Even when she shoved her hands in her pockets and discovered her wand there. Normally, this would be the cue to grip that twig and pull it into the open, ready to wave it at whatever was causing her distress. But today, she was more interested in the boiled sweet that sat beneath it, stuck to the pocket lining.

After freeing the sweet, she sucked it and listened.

Stories were being shared.

'Practically the whole street is infested. Libby Woodhouse's mum found twenty-nine of them munching on a Victoria sponge she'd baked.'

'Little Robyn Gee went to put some bread in her toaster when a mouse popped out from inside and ran off with it. It's a wonder the beast didn't ask for butter and jam at the same time.'

'How badly is school infested?'

'They're in the classroom . . .'

'And the gym . . .'

'They've even nibbled through the wires inside the piano.'

'It's going to take a mousetrap the size of Seacross to catch all the blighters. And lord knows how much it'll cost in cheese to tempt them in.'

It was all a bit surreal.

'Can this week get any stranger?' Kay asked herself. With Dad hallucinating and Wilf's wizarding looming larger than ever, she doubted it could, and she felt a confusing mixture of unease and excitement surge through her.

She knew she should race home, keep safe, check on Dad, but in her eyeline she could also see Wilf's house and she wondered how the old man was.

Home or Wilf's? Home or Wilf's?

It should have been an easy decision to make; she could hear Dad's voice telling her so. But as his insisting grew louder in her ears, Wilf emerged from his front door, staff in hand and bag on back. What was he doing on his feet so quickly, after everything that had happened that morning?

He was clearly off on another magical mission: one Kay couldn't afford to miss. Not if she wanted to be sure about the strength of his powers. So, without hesitation, she bolted in the old man's direction, yelling his name as she went.

Just the Two of Us

'Ah, my friend!' Wilf beamed as Kay bounded up. 'The mountain lion. Shouldn't you be prowling into school, or savaging wildebeest?'

'Nah,' Kay answered. 'School's closed. Mice everywhere. Not just there, either. Storey Street's full of them, apparently.'

The old man looked surprised. 'Really? No sign of any in my place.'

'Funny that,' Kay grinned, thinking about the army of kittens behind his front door. 'Can't think why!'

'So if you have no school, Kay Catt, then you must join me. We're on a mercy mission. There are lives to save and I could use a fearless warrior like you.'

Kay giggled. She'd been called a lot of things in her life but fearless and a warrior weren't two of them. It was enough of a compliment to see her breathe deep and swallow enough fear to set off with Wilf in the direction of the canal.

Progress was slow. The old man's movements were stiff, like a tin man who'd taken hourly showers with no towel to dry himself off. But although reduced to a shuffle, Wilf moved with a smile on his face.

'Today is going to be a good day, I can tell.' He beamed.

'Can't get any worse, can it?'

'Oh, I don't know about that. What's wrong with today?'

Kay looked at Wilf quizzically. 'Er, depends if you see being set on fire as a positive or not?'

'Oh, that!' he chuckled. 'Can't be helped. I'm sure it was simply a case of high spirits from the young gentlemen. I'm sure they didn't mean to barbecue me like a burger.'

Kay wasn't so sure. 'Wilf . . . ?' she asked. 'Why did you let them bully you like that? You know, when you're so powerful and all?'

He stared at her, eyes glinting with life despite their age.

'My dear, what an excellent question! Though surely you know the answer. You are pretty powerful too, yet you let them treat you the same way!'

Kay would've laughed if she hadn't been so confused. Comparing her power with Wilf's was like comparing a pedalo with the *Titanic*!

Yet, when she told him so, he simply said, 'Piffle and poppycock!' which ended the conversation immediately and confusingly for Kay, so she changed tack.

'Do you think the incident would've happened if you didn't dress so . . . you know . . . extravagantly?'

Wilf looked at her over his half-moon specs, impressed by her word power, before staring at his cloak.

'What, this old thing? I'd hardly call this extravagant. You should see me in my Sunday best. I look quite the dandy. I turn heads 360 degrees!'

'But you have to admit, you do attract attention, dressing like you do.'

'And is that a problem? Can't an old man dress to impress?'

Kay shook her head. It wasn't a problem to her; she loved the way he looked.

'I just wish people weren't so cruel,' she said, 'because you dare to be different.'

'My dear old thing. If people stop, or stare, or point, or laugh, don't for one second think that it upsets me. Quite the opposite. You must flip that thought upside down and shake it by the ankles.'

'What do you mean?

'I, my dear, am an old, old man. There are great oaks younger than me. And old men are of no interest to anyone or anything. Now, I'm not looking for your sympathy, far from it. But as you get older and less interesting, it's not just your own eyesight that fades. It is the eyesight of others around you. People fail to notice you any more: they fail to see how you could be of any use. And as a result, you cease to exist. So if wearing a hat and cloak brings me back to life, then I'm very happy with that.'

'In that case, I wish I was old. I'd do anything to be invisible. Might stop people looking at me like I'm a weirdo.'

'Oh no no no. Lions can never be invisible. That's the whole point. As soon as they walk in a room, everyone knows they're there. They command the space! You can't be a king and be invisible!'

'I wish I understood what you meant with this lion stuff.' She blushed, feeling foolish. 'I don't know what it means, so I don't know how to believe in it.'

Wilf tapped his temple with his staff. 'Think like a pussycat and people will feed you kippers. But think like a lion, and you'll be feasting on steak for as long as you live!'

'Do you ever speak in anything that isn't a riddle?'

'Are you kidding?' Wilf said with a smile. 'Have you ever heard of a wizard who doesn't? Dumbledore would've been a dullard if he didn't speak like he did. And don't get me started on that Gandalf. Have you ever listened to him?'

Of course Kay had. She'd read every word and watched every minute of every film. And Wilf spoke just like him. It was all Kay needed to hear.

Everything she thought about Wilf was true – it had to be. She was friends with a wizard and she blooming well loved it.

The old man pulled his staff from the water with a flourish, bringing with it a brown sack that had been nestled amongst the weeds.

'What's that?' she asked. 'Is it . . . what I think it is?' Kay asked.

'I'm rather afraid it might be,' Wilf said, pulling the bag from the hook and opening it gingerly. 'Help me down, would you, my dear?'

With great care, Kay took Wilf's arm as he knelt on the ground, spreading the sack wide to reveal a helpless, lifeless, matted bundle of fur.

'Is it . . . you know?' Kay couldn't bring herself to say the word.

'Not if we can help it,' Wilf answered, leaning forward and wrapping his hands around the kitten's chest. From there, the old man proceeded to rock gently backwards and forwards, his hands massaging and probing. As he rubbed and rocked, he bent his head forward, words tumbling gently out of his mouth and into the ear of his patient. Kay craned towards him, trying to make sense of what he was saying, but it was no use. Whatever spell he was weaving, it was between him and the cat.

On Wilf went, massaging and muttering, massaging and muttering.

Seconds dragged into minutes. Wilf kept working. Kay kept worrying. Why was nothing happening? Had the sack been in the canal too long for his magic to work? Kay didn't think she could bear it if that was the case.

On Wilf went, knees creaking, chest rasping with effort, until finally, slowly, his rocking stopped, and he clasped his hands to his chest, head bowed over the bundle.

'Oh no,' Kay gasped, 'please . . .'

Wilf lifted his head, eyes glistening. His hands rose slowly and opened to reveal the kitten laid across his palms, the slightest trace of a heartbeat rippling across its chest, the tiniest meow leaving its mouth.

'You did it!' Kay squealed. 'How did you do that? How did you bring it back?'

But the old man offered no explanation. He looked tired, spent, like his miracle had sucked all energy from his ageing bones. 'Would you like to feed her?'

Kay didn't need any encouragement, and within minutes she was sat on a bench as the kitten lazed on her lap, sucking hungrily at a baby's bottle. *What a gift*, she thought to herself as her eyes went back to Wilf, who was easing out his aching, stiff limbs.

Oh my, she thought, *oh my*. There was magic in him. So much magic.

More than anyone she had ever met.

Panic on the Streets of Seacross

Wilf and Kay walked on to Storey Street covered in triumph, striding along like two Roman gladiators. Well, if gladiators wore burnt wizard's capes and carried a snoring kitten. Anyway, they looked like a couple of winners. Let's leave it at that and move on, shall we?

They planned a celebration as only they knew how: with drum, bass and dancing cats, but as their disco loomed closer, their ears were bombarded with a very different kind of music. In fact, it wasn't music at all: it was screaming. Verse after verse and chorus after chorus of high-pitched wailing that threatened to burst every eardrum in the north of England.

'What's going on?' asked Kay, wishing she could wear the sleeping kitten in her arms like a fashionable and effective pair of earmuffs.

'I have no idea,' said Wilf, pulling his oversized hat down over his lobes.

It didn't take long however for all to become clear, for as they passed the windows of the chip shop, Oh My Cod, and the Chinese takeaway, Wokever You Want, they saw the same thing.

Mice.

Hundreds of them, fighting over chips and pork balls, ripping open sachets of vinegar and hoisin sauce. It was like a fast food turf war.

But it wasn't just confined to the shops: it was the houses too. Every place they passed told the same story. There were mice on the windowsills, mice in the window boxes; they were streaming out of letter boxes and underneath garage doors. Kay even

spotted them dancing on the roofs like rodent chimney sweeps.

It was more than an infestation, it was an invasion, and no number of brooms and spades being waved could ease the problem.

With every passing minute, panic grew: it was like watching ants streaming from their hills, but with sharper teeth and way more germs.

'What are we going to do?' yelled Lucie Biggs, waving a dustpan and brush as she stood on her car bonnet.

'I've no idea,' answered her husband George, who was a hulking ex-wrestler, but was currently quivering on the car's

roof, brandishing a vacuum cleaner that wasn't even plugged in. 'I tried to call Rentokil but they've no mouse traps left. And besides, the corner shop's run out of cheese to put on them.'

It was the same story everywhere they looked: families in crisis, huddled together on work surfaces and chairs as rodents tormented them from below. Who knew where it would end? How long would it be before the mice took over and started running the show, demanding breakfast in bed, bigger wages and longer holidays in the summer?

The only person on Storey Street who wasn't panicking was Wilf Wilkinson.

Kay was, though, her skin crawling like a baby who'd spotted a chocolate biscuit on the other side of the room.

'My dear Kay. Do you remember that thing I said, about being invisible to everyone?

Kay nodded.

'Well, I do believe it may be time to reverse that. How do you feel about us becoming the most popular people in Seacross history?'

Kay trusted Wilf. More than anyone she'd ever met, but at the same time she knew his plan would make her palms sweat.

'Live a little,' Wilf added. 'Be like me. I'll try anything once, though I draw the line at eating sprouts. They look like enormous freeze-dried bogeys.'

Kay smiled nervously, the thought of sprouts, bogeys and mysterious plans forming a mush in her brain.

Wilf, however, was feeling no fear. He marched towards home with only one thought in his head.

This was going to be epic.

Panic on the streets of Seacross. Yells, screams and endless thwacks of mousetraps snapping unsuccessfully. Residents were packing suitcases, burning belongings in bin fires – it was the very definition of chaos.

Matters weren't helped either when a wrinkly old man in ridiculous clothes was spotted climbing on to the roof of a car, whilst a shy-looking girl stood beneath him, clutching a battered old ghetto blaster.

'Ladies and gentlemen!' the old man shouted in a surprisingly loud voice. 'Don't be afraid. I bring good news. The mice will soon be gone. Trust in me! I will not let you down!'

Without hesitation, without waiting for the inevitable cries of 'Shut up, you plonker!' from the non-believers, he instructed the girl to hit 'play' on the stereo system, and the air was filled with the sickest, bassiest beats the small seaside town had ever heard.

'I hardly think this is time for dancing,' yelled Lucie Biggs.

'Turn it off!' yelled others.

But their pleas weren't heard. It was impossible to hear anything over the music. George Biggs took matters into his own hands, jumping from his place of safety and walking over to Kay.

'Please!' he begged. 'This isn't helping anyone, is it? What are you trying to do? Disco them to death?'

'It'll be OK, Mr Biggs,' said Kay. 'Please, you have to trust Wilf. Watch!'

Now, George Biggs wasn't a horrible man. Far from it. He was kind and gentle, despite his huge frame, but he'd just about had enough today. He'd already found a dozen mice swimming breaststroke in his bath, and the little blighters had nibbled through every pair of underpants he owned. So he could be forgiven for not wanting a rave to break out in his street.

But as he lunged for the stereo, his eye was grabbed by the most incredible sight.

Kittens. Not one, playing innocently with a ball of wool, but a legion of them, pouring out of the front door of a shabby terraced house at the far end of Storey Street.

George looked away, then looked back. It was astonishing. There were so many it looked like a furry patchwork carpet was rolling its way towards them.

'What the Dickens is going on?' George asked.

Within seconds, a hundred kittens of varying size had congregated in the middle of the road, waiting expectantly as the old man drove his staff on to the car roof three times. Obediently, the kittens sat like docile Labradors begging for treats.

'More volume!' the old man asked of his assistant, before throwing his arms into the air like a conductor. What happened next took some believing, as one by one the kittens lifted themselves on to their back legs and started to bust some serious moves.

'Hang on a second,' said Lucie Biggs, who wondered if she'd mistakenly eaten some cheese with hallucinatory qualities. 'Are those cats dancing?'

'Er . . . looks like it,' answered her son, Jake. 'Unless we're all asleep and having the same freaky dream.'

Up and down Storey Street, reactions were the same: disbelief and incredulity.

How was this happening? And, more importantly, why?

Kay watched their faces, recognising the emotions she'd had the first time she'd seen Wilf in action, and feeling pride that he was now her friend.

Stepping gingerly from the car to the road, the old man and his apprentice forged a path through the mambo-ing moggies and led them to the very end house, where they asked the owners for permission to enter.

They were unable to object (as their mouths failed to work), so the unlikely flash mob poured through the front door, the music muffled slightly as the stereo moved deep inside the house.

A crowd gathered by the front gate. Was the old man a genius or a cunning robber who was going to steal every trinket that lay inside? It was possible. Anything was on a day as bonkers as this one.

But just as residents thought about locking up their jewellery boxes, the front door re-opened and a sea of mice fled out, followed quickly by a torrent of cats.

It was a sight to behold, like the most extreme episode of *Tom and Jerry* ever made. The cats might not have been dancing any more, but they were still having one heck of a time. At the rear, Wilf appeared, clearly energised by his army, and drove them on with cheers and encouragement.

'To the end of the road!' he yelled against the music. 'There's a drain that leads to the canal.'

Now, I have no idea if kittens can truly understand human orders, especially when they're hungrily chasing prey and dancing, but I'll be darned if those hundred kittens didn't do exactly what the wizard told them.

Without hesitation, and with great joy, they scampered on, driving the mice like miniature sheep until they hit the end of Storey Street and disappeared like dirty bath water down the storm drain.

More noise erupted, but this wasn't a new, even louder dance tune: this was applause and cheers and relief, pouring from the people of Storey Street.

He might have only cleared one infested house so far, but in five short minutes, Wilf Wilkinson had gone from wacky weirdo to supreme saviour. And as for his assistant? Well, young Kay Catt was being lauded too.

It was a new feeling for her, to feel brave, and strong, and boy oh boy, did it feel good.

Wizard Wilf Wows 'Em

Popularity is a funny thing. Not 'funny ha-ha' like when someone breaks wind in the middle of a Maths exam. I mean, that *is* funny, until it starts to stink and the windows won't open.

No, popularity is more 'funny weird'. Take Wilf Wilkinson and his nervy companion Kay for example. Ask anyone about them twenty minutes before I typed this and they'd have called them the following:

Weirdos

Plonkers

Barnpots

Wasters

And these are the kinder of the insults. There were some that were so unpleasant and rude that I thankfully don't know how to spell them. And besides, even if I did, my mum would tell me off if I put them in the pages of this book.

Let's just say that previously, Wilf and Kay weren't popular. But now, after their moggy militia rid the first house of mice, they were more in demand than the tooth fairy in a town where children's diets consist of hundred-year-old sticks of rock.

'Wilf?' they cried, one after the other. 'Sir? Would you help us?'

'The mice have eaten all our food . . .'

'All our cupboards . . .'

'They've eaten the corner of our fridge . . .'

'And my eldest son!'

It was sob story after sob story, each one more grand and unbelievable than the one before. Thankfully, Wilf wasn't a cynical old man. Far from it: his heart was as huge as his clothes were flamboyant.

'Good lord,' he whispered as he turned to Kay. 'Look how popular we seem to be!'

'You don't have to help *everyone*, you know, not if you're too tired,' Kay answered with a smile, feeling happier than she had in a long, long time. 'There are more mice than there are people in the whole town!'

'Well, we can't have that, can we? We must weave our magic, my mountain lion, and banish these evil spirits to the underworld!'

'Or at least to the storm drain at the end of the road,' Kay added.

'Well, quite,' said Wilf, 'but who knows where *that* leads.' And he turned to the crowd.

'My friends, please don't worry. I will not leave you in your time of need. As long as there is magic in my bones, batteries in my stereo . . . and milk in my kittens' bellies, then we will work on. These mice will not beat us. They will NOT PASS!'

And thonking his staff energetically on to the pavement like Gandalf the Grey after a lie-in and a full English breakfast, he moved on to the next house, his loyal moggies congregating around him.

The results were no less impressive the second time around, or indeed the third and fourth. Music pulsed and kittens boogied, bopped and drove mouse after mouse down the length of Storey Street.

It was surreal to watch, like nothing you'd ever seen in your life, but with every house they cleared, Wilf seemed to grow in stature. He did not tire or ask for a break, but at the same time he didn't refuse cups of tea or slices of cake, either (as long as the sugary treats had been hidden from the mice in stainless steel tins).

Wilf had a particularly sweet tooth and found it impossible to turn down anything that was offered. It made Kay wonder when he'd last eaten a proper meal.

'This must be why Father Christmas works at night,' he said. 'That way he can turn down the occasional mince pie without offending anyone.'

'Maybe we should be dancing with the cats,' Kay answered. 'Might stop us from feeling quite so full!'

On the pair worked, adding in the occasional shimmy and shake as they moved from house to house, though Wilf's dancing was not as magical as his kitten training.

Three hours on and one whole side of Storey Street was vermin-free. Five hours on and there were only two houses left to deal with.

'Should we give the kittens another rest?' worried Kay, but Wilf shook his head and pointed at them, still dancing more energetically than a breakdancer who'd been struck by lightning and injected with liquid doughnuts.

So, with gusto, the kittens ploughed on, surging and searching and sniffing out their foes, taking the most obscene delight in hounding them from every shadowy corner they could find. Fifteen minutes and one hundred and thirty-one mice later, there was only one residence left to inspect, and that belonged to Mr A. Catt, and his daughter, Kay.

Mouse Hunters . . .

Kay felt conflicted about stepping inside with their crowd of kittens. If Dad was still burning up with a fever, the last thing his brain would cope with was a horde of dancing cats on his duvet. It could be the thing that pushed him over the edge. And besides, she'd not spotted any evidence of mice anywhere.

'Do you not think we should have a look, though?' asked Wilf. 'Seems unlikely your house would be clear when everyone else has been infested. And besides, I would LOVE to meet your father.'

'I wouldn't get too excited,' mumbled Kay, as she threw the idea around in her head. Her dad certainly wouldn't want to meet Wilf.

What should she do? Turn the stereo down a bit and hope to get the job done without waking Dad up?

But what if he was already awake? What if the mice had abducted him in his weakened state? Or chewed through the floorboards, leaving his bed in the lounge instead of upstairs?

Kay felt a pulse of anxiety spread through her body, rippling down to her toes and all the way up to the ends of her hair. She didn't like it. Not one bit. It creased her forehead and addled her thoughts.

'Could we do it quietly?' she asked Wilf. 'Without waking him up?'

'We'll be quiet as mice,' he answered, before realising what he'd said. 'Well, you know what I mean.'

Turning down the stereo to a volume acceptable in a library, Kay pulled out her front door key and pushed inside. It was quiet, only the humming of the fridge breaking the silence.

Wilf burst into action, dispatching his troops with a whisper and a silent wave of his staff. Off they scampered to every part of the ground floor, sniffing and scratching at any door that needed opening.

But, five minutes on, they returned with nothing. Not a mouse, not a rat – not even a spider that had been weaving a holiday home in the cupboard under the sink.

'Strange,' said Wilf, pulling at his beard. 'Curious.'

'Perhaps we just got lucky,' Kay added. 'Or maybe they heard about my dad. Heard he was a bit . . . highly strung.'

Wilf was not open to such wild theories, however, telling Kay firmly that they must venture upstairs. 'Just a quick look, to be sure.'

Stealthily, Wilf led their army up, up, up, Kay's heart thudding louder than the kittens' paws on the wooden steps.

'Start in the bathroom,' she whispered, and Wilf obliged, though they discovered nothing. Nor did they in Dad's study, or Kay's room, though Wilf did pause to pick up the photo at the top of the stairs. It was so packed with warmth and adoration that he smiled and fixed Kay with a look of sheer love.

'Ah,' he said, 'a pride of lions. Magnificent. There is no finer sight.' And with great care, he placed the photo back on the table and led the way back into the hall.

'Right,' whispered Kay. 'Just Dad's room to do. Let me go in first, will you? 'Cos if there's no sign of a mouse then there's no point you following. Always let a sleeping dad lie . . . or something like that.'

Palms sweating, she pushed the bedroom door ajar, eyes adjusting to the shadows. Dad's duvet had slithered to the floor in a heap, leaving Kay to think, *Dad's wearing new pyjamas. They aren't stripey like his normal ones.*

She strained against the light. They were definitely different. They seemed to have an animal print on them. But what animal was it? Sheep? Kay looked closer. No, they weren't woolly. Dogs, then? Nope, the tails were longer and thinner. So what were they? Kay leant in, her nose almost touching Dad. It was only then that she recoiled in fear and disgust. That wasn't an animal pattern at all. They were *real* flipping animals, using Dad's radiator-like heat as a place to snooze. Dad was covered, from neck to ankle, in dozing, dozy MICE!

'Oh no, oh no, oh no oh no oh no.'

This was a nightmare, a living, breathing feature film of a nightmare, shot in 3D and shown on IMAX.

There was no way she could clear the room without the help of the kittens, but how could they work quietly enough without waking him up?

Ideas stewed in her head like a tea bag, but none of them were any good. All she could see was failure.

Hoping that Wilf might throw her a lifeline, she tried to creep back to the hall. But, in doing so, she leant on a squeaky floorboard, which wailed, prompting a groan and a roll from Dad – which in turn woke one hundred and sixty-three mice from their delicious slumber. That movement prompted interest from the kittens in the doorway, who, spotting the mice, tore into the bedroom to chase them, waking the rest of the rodents in the process.

Oh my giddy aunt. You should've seen the carnage. I'd try and describe it for you, but I'm rubbish at adjectives, so *look* at the madness instead!

It was bonkers. Terrified mice, crazed kittens, an elderly wizard who tried to restore control by turning up the stereo – which only succeeded in finally waking Dad, who thought he'd crossed into a terrible parallel universe.

'URGNHGHNNNNNBRRRGGHHHHH!' he wailed, which translated into 'Oh my days, I'm covered in MICE!'

It didn't take him long to clamber off the mattress and crouch upon the headboard, which clearly wasn't built for a man of his size. It creaked and cracked like a branch being squatted on by a buffalo, and within seconds it disintegrated, starting a domino effect that saw the whole bed frame collapse to the floor.

The noise was astonishing, enough to terrify the mice into a hasty retreat. The kittens followed them along the hall, down the stairs and back out the front door, leaving Dad, Kay, Wilf and a blaring stereo back in the bedroom.

'There . . . were . . . mice . . .' Dad mouthed, his every pore sweating. 'And . . . kittens. Lots and lots . . . of kittens.'

'There were,' Kay said, 'but they're gone now.'

'But there's a strangely dressed old man too. And why does he like such terrible music?'

Kay thought about how to answer this without sounding like a right wally. 'This is Wilf, Dad. He's the wizard I told you about. He's here to help.'

Wilf turned the stereo down before stepping forward and offering Dad his bony hand.

Dad paused, head processing at a fevered rate. He looked emotional, then relieved, then confused, before settling on something resembling volcanic.

'What is going on around here? Is this the man you told me about? The *wizard?* Look at him, Kay! Look at him. He's clearly a wicked old fraud!'

'He's not wicked!' Kay answered, feeling tearful. 'He's not. He's my friend. And he is a wizard! The most powerful one on the planet. Tell him, Wilf!'

Wilf's mouth opened, but no words came out, no matter how hard he tried.

'Please, Wilf, please. Tell him.'

Wilf's head dropped a touch, then a touch more, until he lost all eye contact. Until he just looked . . . old.

Kay was starting to feel frantic. She shuffled from foot to foot, ignoring the tears that pricked behind her eyes.

'Tell him what you can do, Wilf. Tell him about the cats. About the spells that make them dance. About how you bring them back to life. Because he can, Dad, I saw him do it.'

The old man pulled his glasses from his face and rubbed at his eyes like he needed to sleep for ever.

Kay was confused. What was he doing? Why wasn't he putting Dad straight?

'I need you to tell him, Wilf. I need him to know the truth. To know what I know. You're my best friend, Wilf, so tell him, please!'

But it didn't matter how hard or loud she begged, Wilf said nothing. Instead, he looked despairingly at his young friend, tears rolling down his creased, wrinkled face.

'Oh, my dear old thing,' he wept. 'Nothing would give me greater joy . . . but I can't do that. I wish I was what you want me to be, more than anything. But I'm not. Not quite. And I'm . . . I'm . . . sorry.'

At that moment, Kay's world collapsed. Every bit of hope that had built tentatively inside her crumbled and fell to her feet.

'But you dress like a wizard . . .'

Wilf nodded. That much was true.

'And you have the beard and the specs and the staff . . . and I've seen what you can do. I saw you bring on the thunderstorm, and make the cats dance. I saw you bring that kitten back to life!'

The old man sighed, a sad smile flickering across his lips. 'Sometimes I just get lucky . . .'

'No, it's more than that, I saw it with my own eyes! It's magic.'

'We all have gifts, my dear. Talents. You have them too. You made an old man happy for the first time in years. When my Wilma died, I thought I'd never feel anything again. Nothing good, anyway. And, for a long time, I didn't. I felt invisible, like I wasn't really here. That's why I wear this.' He pointed at his cloak. 'It belonged to her. She was magical, my Wilma, and she believed in things – out of this world things. So I thought if I believed too, well, I thought I could keep her alive. And I've tried. I've tried so hard. To be different, and special, but the truth is, I'm no wizard. Lucky, maybe. Good with animals, certainly. But a wizard? I'm not, and I'm sorry.'

Kay felt crushed. Like someone had taken her heart and squeezed it like a grapefruit. But she also felt a new emotion, one that she neither recognised nor liked.

She felt anger.

'How could you do this to me, Wilf?' she sobbed. 'How could you lie to me like this? I trusted you. I was brave because of you. I felt like I could be brave because I thought you'd protect me. But it was all a lie. So you're not my friend at all, are you?'

'Of course I am,' Wilf cried, stepping forward, only to see Kay recoil. 'And you *are* brave.' He looked to her dad for support. 'Do you know how brave your daughter is, Mr Catt? Did you know she is, in fact, a lion?'

Dad looked understandably confused.

'I'm sorry?'

'Your daughter. It might not be clear to you, but unless I'm very much mistaken, and I very rarely am, your daughter is a mighty mountain lion.'

Dad shook his head, trying to rid himself of the madness. 'I think you'd better go now.'

'It may sound bizarre, but I promise you it's true. There is more bravery and more spirit in that girl's index finger than there is in all the other children on this street. One day soon you'll see, Mr Catt, I promise you. One day soon you will see her in action, fierce and brave, and when you see her – when you hear her roar – then you'll understand. And you won't feel scared. Not for her, and not for yourself. How could you when you live with a lio—'

'Stop it!' Kay cried, tears streaming down her face. 'You can't say that to me. It isn't true, and I will not listen. Not any more.'

She felt an arm on her shoulder. Dad's arm. Not to overprotect her for once, but to comfort her.

'Oh, Mr Catt,' said Wilf. 'I apologise profusely. To both of you. You are a magical girl, Kay, the most magical I've ever me—'

'I think it's time you left. I want you to. And Kay does too. Isn't that right, Kay?'

Oh, my dear reader. It breaks my heart to tell you this, just as it broke Kay's heart too, but our little heroine felt like she had no option but to nod.

She couldn't be around her friend. Not any more.

All she could do was look at her shoes as she heard the old man shuffle down the path.

The shuffling got softer, and softer, until soon it had gone, leaving only the sound of her pounding, broken heart.

Dad Digs In

Magic went missing from Kay's life very quickly. Quicker than you could say 'abracadabra'.

It was replaced by drudgery (a posh word for hard and dull work) and the all-consuming ball of anxiety that was Dad. It wasn't helped by the fact that school remained closed too, as Wilf and Kay hadn't managed to weave their magic there before being halted. So, while school was fumigated, Dad became both her private teacher and headmaster.

He didn't mean to make Kay's life so hard – the poor man was still recovering from flu for starters – but his every move, his every decision was based on fear. Even his lessons were.

'Read this passage about grizzly bears, Kay, and list for me the numbers of ways that they are dangerous . . .'

'If the first earthquake measures 5.1 on the Richter scale, and the second measures 4.8, what is the force of the two earthquakes combined, and what should you do if one hits?'

It wasn't exactly textbook teaching, not unless the textbook was called *Teaching by Terrification: How to Scare your Child to an 'A' Grade*.

And you know what? It had quite an effect on Kay. Gone were the blossoming feelings of bravery and hope: back were the usual feelings of fear and anxiety. Oh, and sadness, too. Lashings and lashings of sadness.

She thought of Wilf a lot, even though she didn't want to. She was angry with him, of course she was. She felt foolish, and lied to, and foolish. But every time he popped into her head, it wasn't an image of a cruel, fibber of a man, but a smiley, big-hearted one.

'Stop it,' Kay would grimace. 'Leave me alone, Wilf. Leave me be.' And she'd pour her attention back into completing Dad's homework: a word search consisting of ways to die accidentally.

It wasn't the cheeriest of exercises and Kay couldn't find 'electrocution' no matter how hard she looked.

In fact, as the days rolled on, she became more and more distracted. And she thought of Wilf more and more too.

Magician or mortal, he had been her friend.

It may hurt that the old man wasn't capable of casting a spell or two, but she missed so much about him.

His wondrous sideways look at the world, and how he massaged things back to life instead of suffocating them. She missed being a mountain lion, as well as being called one. She wondered if Wilf missed her too.

She kept her eye out for him as she worked at the desk in her bedroom window, but his door never seemed to open, not even when people walked up to it carrying gifts, a steaming pie or hotpot for him and a whole salmon or bottle of cream for the cats.

How Kay wished he'd open his door just once. For her own peace of mind, but for a whole load of other reasons too. She knew Wilf was lonely and poor – he'd admitted as much – so he needed the neighbours' help. It can't have been cheap feeding so many kittens, and from the look of his ancient microwave he didn't seem like much of a chef. Aside from cake, she'd never seen a crumb of food pass his lips.

With each passing day Wilf's absence in her life grew stronger. She wanted to get a message to him, but couldn't find a way to swallow her pride. She'd said such horrid things, had seen the hurt on his face.

What if she never saw him again? And even if she did, what if he didn't want anything to do with her?

Kay had no idea which was worse, but she knew both made her feel, well, terrible.

In times of need, you can always rely on your family to pull you through.

Kind of.

Sort of.

Kay's dad tried his best, his *absolute* best, but each time fell short.

He threw a movie night, but not until he'd watched the films first to check there was nothing unsuitable or scary in them.

He made a bowlful of popcorn, which he then chopped up to minimize the choking risk ('popcrumbs', anyone?). He even bought a bottle of Coke, left open all afternoon to get rid of the fizz. Burping put strain on the heart, and that would never do.

And as for the film itself, well, there certainly weren't any wizards in it.

It's fair to say that by the end Kay felt *pretty* depressed and excused herself to bed, despite it only being 6.42 p.m.

Sitting at the desk in her window, head in hands, she looked intently down the street.

There was no sign of Wilf.

There had been fewer visitors at his door too. People had stopped bringing gifts when he didn't accept their earlier efforts, which made Kay both sad and worried.

OK, of course it was devastating that Wilf wasn't the magical being she thought he was, and of course it hurt like crazy that he couldn't do the things she'd dreamt he could. But once the shock died down, she was still left with a Wilf-shaped hole in her life.

Was he OK in there? Was he looking after himself? Did he have any food whatsoever in the house to feed himself, let alone his cats?

All she could do was sit and watch, day after day, confused by the occasional visitors to Wilf's front door. Visitors that *weren't* neighbours.

In fact, they were anything but.

Knock Knock, Who's there...?

It didn't happen a lot at first, but after a day or two, Wilf's new visitors became a regular occurrence.

It always started the same way, with a white van pulling up outside. A van which held on average two large, strong men – men who looked like they could carry a settee by balancing it on their little finger.

They would close the van doors with an almighty thud before clomping to the front door, where they'd knock with the most incredible ferocity.

It sometimes took a while for Wilf to answer (Kay hoped he was dancing happily inside with the music turned up loud), but these men didn't care. They would wait and knock and wait and knock until the old man answered.

This is the bit where Kay got confused, because the men would immediately flash a sheet of white paper before pushing inside, leaving Wilf to follow helplessly.

Kay would wait a few anxious minutes until the men appeared again, lugging as many boxes as possible, some of which looked pretty heavy. Wilf always remained dejectedly on the doorstep as they drove away, before shepherding any kittens back inside.

Kay spent a lot of time trying to work out what the men were taking, and as the days went by and more and more men appeared, she thought about it even more.

Maybe Wilf had finally agreed to get rid of some of his clutter. To charity maybe?

And if he had, then why was he looking so glum about it? Fewer boxes meant more space, which meant a bigger dance floor, which meant happier kitte— *Of course!* Kay thought to herself, slapping her forehead for not thinking of it earlier.

There were kittens in the boxes! Wilf must have made the painful decision that he couldn't look after them all, especially as they grew into cats, and was slowly giving them away.

Although this made Kay feel sad for her friend, it also summed up how generous he was. Imagine how many families he was going to make happy by giving away his moggie mates. Dozens and dozens of them, hundreds maybe.

His generosity made her miss Wilf even more. Made her feel even more foolish for thinking so ill of him.

She wanted to apologise more than anything, but her shame felt overwhelming, too great to carry.

Storey Street felt a million miles long, and boy, did that give Kay Catt the blues.

Happiness comes in many shapes and sizes. To some people it looks like a chocolate egg as big as an elephant's head. To others it's an email telling you you're entitled to a million-zillion pounds, if you just send a cheque for fifty grand first.

To Kay Catt, happiness arrived in her front garden in the

shape of a telegram. Do you even know what a telegram is? It's a bit like a text message. People used to send them before phones were invented, back when people were too thick and lazy to invent cool technology.

Anyway, Kay was working in her bedroom window when the air was split by a sick, kicking beat. Kay felt her heart kick back and her eyes widen in excitement. This kind of awesome bassline could only mean only one thing. Wilf had come out of hibernation. Her eyes roamed the length of the street, but she could see no sign of him. Not a peek of his beard from behind a lamp post, nor his bent hat from above a car bonnet.

But just as Kay dismissed it as a cruel joke, she saw the most wonderful thing: an endless stream of furballs marching towards her front gate.

One by one, they filed into her garden, forming a large square around the corners of the lawn. Kay's mind fizzed at the possibilities that could follow, though there was still no sign of Wilf.

As the final kitten stood to attention, the music stopped momentarily, before WHAM! A new, rapid tune shook the foundations of Storey Street, prompting the kittens into action, scurrying wildly round the garden, bashing into each other in comedy fashion. Was this Wilf's way of saying sorry? Of injecting some happiness back into her life?

If it was, it was bloomin' well working. Kay was practically dancing on her window ledge, until the music unexpectedly cut out.

Immediately, the kittens stopped dead, and stood, stock-still, each one of them staring up at the window, their eyes wide and smiling. Kay smiled too as it dawned on her what was going on.

They hadn't been dashing round randomly at all. They were sending her a message from Wilf, making large letters with their bodies by grouping tightly together.

Hello Kay Catt, the first message said, the cats holding position long enough for Kay to read it out loud, before a heavy bass sound made them dash into new positions.

The mountain lion

Kay felt her cheeks flush with affection and pride.

Another beat saw the moggies scampering again.

We all miss you

Drumbeat.

I'm sorry

Drumbeat.

I let you down

Another beat, just as Kay shook her head in disagreement.

Looks like we have to move house

What? thought Kay, re-reading furiously in the hope she'd got it wrong.

We have no choice

There was another drumbeat and the kittens scampered to complete the sentence, but as they did so, there was a noise from downstairs: Dad opening the door to put out the recycling, which sent the cats *and* Dad into something of a panic.

With a yelp of shock, twenty-three yoghurt cartons and six newspapers went hurtling into the air, falling like the world's rubbishest confetti.

Cats fled in every direction, leaving Kay to yell 'NOOO! Not before you finish the sentence. Not before I know what's going on!'

But it was no good getting upset. Kay had been left on a cliffhanger and there was nothing she could do about it.

If the message was true, Wilf was leaving.

She'd heard it straight from the horse's mouth. Well, from the cats' bodies.

What she didn't know was why.

And most importantly of all . . . when.

Happy Days Are Here Again

Never in her wildest dreams did Kay think that going back to school could make her happy.

The mere utterance of the word usually made her feel the same as when someone said 'sprouts', 'earwax' or 'stomach bug'.

But not today, oh no, no way!

Today, the grand reopening of school was something to celebrate, for as Kay stepped through her front door, it felt like she could breathe again.

Gone were the confines of her room and Dad's well-meaning but overprotective ways, and in front of her, she hoped, was the potential to bump into Wilf.

Tucking her hands into her pockets, she found her wand, her fingers gripping it instinctively. But she didn't pull it from her pocket as she usually did. Instead she left it there, and chose instead to breathe deeply to calm herself, before turning to Dad.

'I shall miss you today,' he said.

'Mmmm,' Kay replied. I mean, how did you answer that? She loved her dad, but being locked up in a house with him 24/7 while he filed the sharp corners off everything (including loaves of bread) just wasn't fun any more.

She'd rather spend the day being ribbed mercilessly by everyone in class than endure another day being homeschooled.

And besides, the walk to school meant edging closer to Wilf's house, which meant a chance to do some detective work, to try and deduce exactly what yesterday's moggie messages meant.

But as they approached his tatty terrace, another white van pulled up outside: a van very similar to the ones that had visited on previous days. The men driving it looked familiar too, like they'd been hired from a shop called Rent-a-Thug or Buy-a-Bully.

After bailing out of the van, the two men barrelled their way to the front door and knocked ferociously. Kay felt her stride slow. She didn't want to walk past without hearing what the men were after, but Dad was having none of it, pulling her along like a dog who had paused to sniff a particularly interesting dollop of poo.

'Don't be worrying about what's going on there, Kay Catt,'

said Dad. 'Whatever it is, there's nothing you can do to help. He's a grown man, he can deal with it.'

But what was *going on?* Kay asked herself. Were the men really visiting from a charity as she hoped? Was Wilf really donating his wife's old things, or his beloved kittens? The men didn't look like charitable types, not unless the charity was for thugs who'd fallen on hard times after unsuccessful careers terrorising pensioners.

She didn't really believe that Wilf would give away all of Wilma's belongings; he missed her too much for that. And as for the cats, well, that didn't make sense in any shape or form. Why would Wilf give away the things that meant the most to him?

These were the thoughts that dominated Kay's mind as she said goodbye to Dad, her body tense and mind distracted as he told her, rather predictably, to *stay safe* during the day.

Off into school she ambled, pinballing amongst the other kids who were excited to be back. The only positive Kay could find was that from her seat she could clearly see Wilf's front door, allowing her to be some kind of long-distance, slightly ineffectual spy.

It didn't take long for her to do some more deduction, as the shaven-headed henchmen had reappeared outside Wilf's front door, carrying not a series of boxes this time, but his battered-looking armchair and, bizarrely, his ancient, food-spattered microwave. Kay shook her head in confusion. What in the name of Gandalf's underpants did they want with such useless items? Why would anyone buy them, no matter how cheaply Wilf was selling?

Fortunately for Kay, she wasn't the only one keeping her beady eyes on the situation.

'Oh no, see that . . . ?' said Daisy Smith.

'. . . The bailiffs are back at Wizard Wilf's,' finished Liv Smith.

Kay's ears pricked up. What had they just said?

'That's the fifth lot in the last two days . . . my mum said there'll soon be nothing left inside but cobwebs and kittens.'

Danny Christmas leant over from his desk and joined in. 'So sad, isn't it? My dad said we should do something to help, after everything he did with the mice. But if he's so poor that they're taking an old microwave, then what can we really do to help? He must be properly broke.'

Kay felt panic sweep through her body, forcing a cold sweat on to her skin. They couldn't be right, could they? I mean, she'd heard about bailiffs before, coming to take things when people couldn't pay their bills. But it couldn't be that bad for Wilf, surely?

How much must it cost to feed himself and the cats? She did some basic sums on her pad, sweating when she multiplied the price of a can of cat food by the number of kittens under Wilf's roof. The answer was the sort of sum that would bankrupt a banker. Kay gulped, and turned to Liv and Daisy, who she never usually dared to speak to.

'What happens when there's nothing left to take, but there's still a debt to be paid?'

The girls stared at her, in amazement that she'd spoken at all.

'Don't you watch soap operas?' asked Daisy.

'It's obvious,' added Liv. 'Soon as the most expensive item has gone, like a TV, or his stereo, then the only thing they can take is the house itself.'

'How do they *take* the house?' Kay panicked, her brain scrambling.

'They don't literally take it . . . They just kick you out of it.'

Oh sweet lord! Kay thought.

Wilf, homeless? That was too awful to contemplate. She thought about what his most expensive possession would be . . . the stereo! It had to be, and she took some solace from the fact that no stereo had left the premises; she was sure of that as the white van drove away.

While Wilf could still play music in his house, then she knew he was safe.

Her heartbeat dropped slightly, down to the levels of an elephant who had just run the hundred metres in three seconds flat.

And that's when another white van turned on to Storey Street . . . and there were no prizes for guessing where it stopped.

A Catt on a Hot Tin Roof

Kay felt like she was living inside an oven in the middle of the Sahara whilst wearing a ski suit and eating a curry. Yep, she was burning up with fear.

It was 2.34 p.m., a mere thirty-six minutes from the end of school, but it felt like there was still a triple marathon to run.

No work had been done. Her exercise book was blank and the lid remained tightly on her pen. For the past five hours, she had undertaken only one task, a very long game of I spy, but with slightly new rules, as the only thing Kay had her beady eye on was something beginning with B – for bailiffs.

There had been two more unexpected visits, which resulted firstly in the removal of Wilf's TV, an old heavy box of a thing that looked like it could only receive two channels in black and white.

It disturbed Kay how broke Wilf must have been if the debt collectors saw the value in repossessing such a relic, and it disturbed her even more that every van that arrived was a different one. How many companies did Wilf owe money to?

The second visit was a heartbreaking one, though, as after much wrangling and finger-pointing the men left not with the stereo, but with Wilf's robe and hat. She might have been seventy metres away, but she could still see her friend sag as the men carried them away.

It was enough to make our heroine boil like a kettle. How dare they take the clothes off an old man, and burnt clothes at that! I mean, what use was a singed cloak? Couldn't they come up with something else to tell their boss? Say that he'd moved, or threatened to turn them into warty toads if they followed through on their threats?

It made her want to jump out of the classroom window and sprint to her friend, to reassure him they could dress him up in a brown sack and put his socks on his ears and he would still be the most magical human on the planet.

But she couldn't, firstly because class hadn't finished and secondly because at that moment, yet *another* van turned on to Storey Street, and yet again stopped flush outside Wilf's front gate.

Kay watched in horror as two more identikit hoodlums walked to the front door, denting it with their gorilla fists. She could've wept as Wilf cowered in the doorway, his hands going to his mouth in shock and despair as they told him what they had come for.

Kay knew without hearing. She desperately didn't want to believe it, but she knew it could only be one thing. The stereo. The thing that animated Wilf's army of little lions.

She felt tears slide down her cheeks as the men wrestled it from Wilf's bare, matchstick arms, not even bothering to return any CDs that might be inside.

A puddle of cats collected at Wilf's feet, their huge eyes radiating sadness and despair. How could daddy allow them to take their music away?

It was all too much to bear, for Wilf, the cats or Kay, and if Liv and Daisy were right, then Wilf had reached the end of the line. The next van would only mean one thing: a life on Seacross's mean streets, living in a cardboard box.

If they could find one with a cat flap.

Kay was pulled from this devastating image by the shriek of the bell. Within seconds she was hammering down the stairs and towards the gates.

She had to find Dad and tell him what she'd seen, what it meant. She had to beg, scream, plead, break wind, do whatever it took to make him see sense and come round to her way of thinking. They had to help Wilf. There was no other option.

Weirdly though, Dad was nowhere to be seen. Not inside or outside the gates. What was she to do? If she dared to leave the premises without him, the consequences would be severe: she'd probably be banished to somewhere horribly remote like the moon, or Antarctica, or Scunthorpe.

But at the same time, if she waited, it might be too late. Who knew when that last fateful van would arrive?

She had to be brave, be a mountain lion, so with a roar only she could hear, she made to race through the gates – only to be yanked back by the hood at the last split second.

'Oh, Kay,' said Miss Maybury. 'Thank goodness. Your dad is stuck in traffic. He's asked me to keep you under lock and ke— I mean, keep you in after-school club. Just till he can get here.'

'It's OK, Miss,' Kay answered desperately. 'I can see myself home. I have a key and everything, and I promise not to turn anything electrical on. I won't even flush the loo, you know, in case a riptide pulls me down the pipe.'

Miss Maybury gave her a confused look. 'I'm sure, dear, but I promised your father I'd keep my eye on you, and the eyes of every other member of staff as well.' And with a grip of iron, she led Kay back to the other end of the playground, past a group of children playing football.

'Not sure your dad would want you joining in there . . .' she said under her breath.

She also passed a gaggle of students skipping and shook her head. She didn't even leave Kay with the knitting club who had congregated in the afternoon sunshine, muttering, 'Knowing my luck she'd take her eye out with a needle.'

It's fair to say that Dad had given Miss Maybury a lecture on his beloved daughter's safety requirements.

Instead, she deposited Kay in the shade with a book that was well below her reading age, so as not to educate her to death, before disappearing inside to fetch her marking.

But Kay was in no mood to read. She was way too agitated. Instead she chewed her nails and watched as the last of the stragglers left the yard and the gates were locked.

'Unbelievable,' she muttered, throwing the book to the ground. She'd been so close to escape, to seeing what she could do to put everything straight.

Instead, she'd merely swapped the prison of home for one at school. It was enough to make her want to scream.

But just as she summoned a roar from the pit of her stomach, she caught sight of something in the corner of her eye. A van. Not a white one this time, but a silver one, with the words 'Deep Pockets Debt Collectors' written on the side.

Kay jumped to her feet and hared to the gates. The van had stopped on the corner of Well Lane, and the driver was hidden behind a large, unwieldy map.

He might have been momentarily lost, but there was no doubt in Kay's mind where the vehicle was going, and what they wanted.

This was it. It had to be. Everything she'd feared, all day long.

But strangely, Kay Catt didn't feel scared.

She felt determined. She felt her inner mountain lion purring.

She had to find a way over the wall. And it didn't take her long to seek out the stout, strong oak in the corner of the playground.

Kay Catt smiled, because she knew two things.

Lions were the kings of the jungle.

And they LOVED to climb trees.

ROOOOOOAAAAAARRRRR

Mountain lions don't have wings. Fact.

Not unless they've been bred in a laboratory by madcap scientists, or unless they live on Storey Street, because I am telling you, Kay Catt *flew* up that oak tree. Hard to believe of a girl usually wracked with fear and anxiety, but true.

One second her feet were on the playground floor, and the next they were dangling in mid air, waiting to drop on to Storey Street.

She should've been nervous – many a brave soul would've been – but Kay had no time or energy for such nonsense. She had to save her pal, and she had to do it quickly, before his house was ripped away from him, and before Dad got home and went ballistic.

Her feet hit the pavement and sprinted across the road, avoiding the ice cream van parked by the curb and the ocean of sugar-hungry post-school students queuing by it. A ninety-nine flake would've been lovely, but it was a luxury she couldn't afford. Wilf's house was a mere twenty metres away, and Kay could feel the engine of the van rasping noisily behind her, getting louder, blowing a raspberry in her ear, telling her they'd get there before her.

She picked up the pace, felt the soles of her feet sizzle like they were on fire. Her lungs weren't far behind.

Only when she reached Wilf's gate did she stop – at the exact same time that three gargantuan geezers heaved themselves from the van's cab. Each of them looked like gorillas who'd been clumsily shaved and wrestled into clothes three sizes too small for them. Kay tried to make herself big, like a boulder blocking the gate, when she looked more like a pebble that any of them could kick across the street.

She copied their stance, thrusting her hands roughly into her pockets, but her left hand was blocked by her wand.

'Ach,' she grunted. She hadn't the time for anything getting in her way. She took the twig and, without thinking, threw it to the ground before her, before turning back to the men.

'Can I help you?' she asked as they approached.

'You live 'ere?' asked the first man.

Kay shook her head.

'Best move, then,' grunted the second.

Kay shook her head again.

'You better had,' frowned the third, which got Kay thinking, mainly about whether they could only speak in sentences that were three words long.

If that was the case, then it would be an irritating conversation.

'This is my friend's house.'

'Not for long,' one of the men replied, which was a sentence that was annoyingly both three words long AND confirmation of Kay's deepest fears.

'He's not in,' Kay blurted, pleased that she had contributed her own three word gem, and hopeful that it might be enough to shoo the men away.

But the bailiffs weren't as believing as Kay was brave.

'Don't believe you,' said one.

'Heard it before,' added the second.

'Yeah, yeah, yeah,' contributed the third, imaginatively.

'I promise you it's true. He was . . . er . . . taken horribly ill this morning. Some sort of tropical disease. Can't even get out of bed. He's covered in warts and is highly contagious. The doctor told me to let no one past. Not if they didn't want to die a painful and warty death.'

It was way more than three words, and way more imaginative, but needs must when bad luck came calling.

'There's no warts.' The first thug pointed.

'Weird-looking, though.'

'Like a wizard.'

Kay turned to see Wilf had opened the door, looking shabby and creased without his cloak and hat.

'Wilf. Close the door and don't answer it till I tell you.'

'What's going on?' he asked.

'Nothing I can't sort out. It'll be fine. Please, just go inside.'

The old man looked confused. So many people had come calling in the last few days, with so many pieces of paper and demands, that he was exhausted. It didn't help that he had no music to occupy the kittens. He could hum a decent tune, but not at the beats per minute they had come to expect.

Obediently, Wilf retreated through the door and closed it with a gentle *snick*.

The heavies were not impressed. So much so that their sentences became a lot more advanced.

'Move out of the way now, Miss.' (Seven words.)

'This is no place for a meddling kid.' (Eight.)

'Especially when it's none of your bloomin', flippin' business.' (Wow, nine!)

But Kay wasn't for budging.

Instead, she crouched slightly, pulling her hands in front of her, whilst curling her fingers into the deadliest of claws. It felt good. Powerful. So powerful that she crunched her mouth into a snarl too.

'Is she growling?'

'Looks like it.'

'Move her on.'

The heaviest thug marched towards Kay, but as his hands neared her, she bared her teeth and let rip with the most ferocious growl.

'She almost bit!' The man scowled.

'For goodness' sake,' replied the second, pushing his way through and ignoring the barking, rabid ten-year-old blocking his path.

Now, Kay wasn't daft. She might have been feeling brave, braver than ever before in her life, but she knew she was no physical match for three men with bulging muscles. Her IQ, however, was triple that of theirs combined, and as the second burly bailiff lifted her into the air, she launched into the next phase of her plan.

Well, when I say plan, that suggests that she'd thought of all this in advance, when actually, she didn't have a Scooby-Doo what to do. She was running on pure adrenalin.

Anyway, the second she was hoisted skywards, Kay gave up on the growling, and started to scream: the loudest, shrillest wail that she could summon from her lungs. A horrible din it was, the combination of a boy-band love song (aaaaarrgghhh) and nails dragging down a blackboard (eeeeeek).

It did little for the eardrums of the three unsuspecting bailiffs, but more importantly, it grabbed the attention of the residents mobbing the nearby ice cream van.

'Put me *down*!' Kay yelped. 'You're hurting me. You're squishing my insides!!'

Kay might have been, until recently, an object of bemusement to some of the people of Storey Street, but most were good, principled folk, who would never stand around as a child's intestines were reduced to icky goo.

Within seconds, three adults, George Biggs, Marvin Mouse and Tony Tipps had broken from the queue and marched upon Wilf's gate. None of them were small men, and as George had once wrestled in Las Vegas, Kay felt a surge of hope in her semi-crushed bones.

'I think you should put that girl down, don't you?' said George, reverting easily into his fighting persona.

'She's in our way.'

Four impressive words, but not enough to make George Biggs applaud. Instead he squeezed himself between the bailiffs and the front gate.

'Looks like I am too, doesn't it?'

'And me,' added Marvin Mouse.

'Me too,' said Tony Tipps.

This is perfect, thought Kay, as the bailiff dumped her on the ground and sized up the three men instead. This bought her time, time to spur the rest of the street into action.

Leaving George and Co. to debate with the bailiffs, Kay dashed in the direction of the ice cream van, grabbing a traffic cone from the road as she ran.

Stopping at the car parked next door, she jumped on the bonnet and clasped the cone to her lips.

'Listen up,' she hollered. 'Please. I need your help. And more importantly, so does Wilf. Now I know you think I'm odd, and I know you think Wilf's even odder. And I suppose we are, but that's not our fault . . . and anyway, it's not even important. What is important, what matters, is that Wilf needs you. He needs you in the same way you needed him a week ago, when those mice were driving you out of your homes. Without Wilf's help you would've been out on the street, and it would've cost a fortune to get your houses back. Now Wilf's in the same position. Those men there, they've come to kick Wilf out, and just like you, he can't stop them unless we help. Unless we line up, next to each other, and don't let them past. So what do you say? Who's with me?'

Kay felt alive. The blood pumped like dance music in her ears. At that moment, she felt more powerful than ever before: she felt like she could hold back the Atlantic Ocean, climb Mount Everest, or eat (in one sitting) a sixty-inch pizza with a triple helping of extra hot chillies and even pineapple (bleurgh).

It seemed, too, that she'd injected life into the ice cream queue. Many of them strode forward: men, women, children, dogs, even a ferret on a lead, forgetting entirely the promise of strawberry sauce and chocolate flakes. The only cone they were hypnotized by wasn't one holding a scoop of vanilla ice cream, but the one that served as Kay Catt's megaphone.

With a raised fist of defiance, Kay led her growing army the short distance to Wilf's house, barking directions as she went.

'That's it. Line up, the whole length of the fence. No, not like

that. There's too big a gap. Link arms, stay together. They must not pass.'

Obediently, the crowd listened. Obediently, they stood strong, not flinching when the bailiffs stopped arguing with George Biggs and noticed what was going on.

'You're kidding me,' they wailed together. What should have been the simplest of jobs was turning into a headache of epic proportions.

They approached the picket line, looking for chinks in its armour. They'd climb over the fence if they had to, but every time they thought they'd found a weakness, the mob closed ranks, squeezing themselves together like the filling in a bacon, egg and sausage sandwich (mmmmm).

At the hub of this impressive resistance was Kay, who prowled amongst the crowd, urging them to be strong, not to budge. She didn't need the megaphone any more. The crowd were with her. Instead, she had the cone perched on her head in honour of Wilf, and as she rallied and encouraged, she hoped her friend was watching proudly.

Which, of course, he was. He was stood at the upstairs window with thirty-four kittens crowded on the ledge around him. And whilst Kay's bravery didn't surprise him one bit, he was taken aback by the amount of support around her.

If the bailiffs went left, the crowd went with them. If they pushed or shoved, the crowd stood strong, never giving an inch. They repelled every movement like an identical magnet. It was the most magical thing Wilf had ever seen in his life.

But it was not over, oh no, not even close.

The bailiffs weren't leaving, not without what they'd come for.

They wouldn't drive away until the old man was sat on the curb, until these irritating idiots had been defeated. So a mere ten minutes after making a phone call, a second van drew up outside, then a third, and fourth.

And from inside emerged the motliest crew, an identity parade of brawn and beefcake. A whole army of aggression.

It was enough to make Kay gulp, to feel a little of her bravery ooze away down the drain. If they were to hold firm, they'd need back-up. But where that was coming from, she had no idea.

When Two Tribes Go To War

So began a tug of war. A tug of war like none before. There was no rope for starters, just two armies, grunting and groaning, not wanting to give a millimetre, not wanting to show weakness.

Kay Catt remained the general, rallying her troops, leading them in song. Not a particularly imaginative song, more like a football chant, albeit one written by a fan with only brain cell.

It consisted of one word, **'Wilf'**, sung at the loudest volume imaginable, but it served as an excellent reminder of who they were fighting for . . . and there was little chance of anyone forgetting the words.

Despite their terrier-like resistance, Kay's foot soldiers started to tire. Little wonder given that some of them were children who'd been denied a life-giving, post-school ice cream.

The bailiffs were like a tribe of slobbering orcs, moving in packs, trying to squeeze through any space that appeared, no matter how small, though it was at times like elephants trying to squeeze through a sieve.

'Stay together! Link arms!' Kay implored, and they obeyed, but it was getting harder. The sieve was in danger of ripping.

We need reinforcements, Kay thought, but she couldn't break ranks to bang on doors to find them. Without her there, who knew how long the barricade would remain intact?

At the far end of the street, though, a flustered, red-faced man was bustling his way toward school. He was late for his daughter, very late, and in his mind, every second counted.

But as the man sprinted up the pavement, he spotted a commotion in his path. It looked like an almighty rugby scrum without a ball, or a tug of war without a r— oh hang on, I did that one already, didn't I?

Whatever it was, he wasn't going to let it delay him any further.

As he drew closer, his eye was drawn to one particular figure, the ringleader as far as he could see, a child little older than his daughter, who for some reason was wearing a traffic cone on her head. She might have looked ridiculous, but the man couldn't take his eye off the child, such was her bravery. The kid was chanting and encouraging and cajoling: there was little doubt that despite her years, she was very much in charge, very much the leader, very much his daugh—

Hang on, he thought.

That girl, with the cone on her head. The brave one, the one risking life and limb, was his daughter. It was Kay.

Arthur felt his organs shrivel up in fear. What on earth was she doing? She should be in school, calmly poring over equations, not leading some kind of revolution.

He couldn't believe it. It was like he didn't recognise her, despite drawing ever closer. Not the fierce look on her face, nor the roar in every word she spoke.

Or did he?

There was actually something about the way she stood, the way she never gave a centimetre, that reminded him of someone else. Someone he'd known very well. Someone he'd loved more than anything.

By the time he reached the throng, he realised it was just like watching his late, great, beloved wife. But saying that, his wife was dead. And that was why he had to protect Kay. He'd never forgive himself if anything happened to her too.

'Kay!' he yelled. She didn't hear. There were too many bodies either groaning or chanting to hear.

'KAY! What are you doing? Come out of there at once!'

The increase in volume was enough to grab Kay's attention, but nowhere near enough to draw her from the battlefield. Not now, not when she'd come so far. She could see his heart thumping through his jumper, but she needed him to see that she could do this. She had to prove to him that there was nothing to be scared of. Not any more.

'Help us, Dad, please. We can't hold them off for ever. And we have to. If they reach the front door they'll evict him. Think of the kittens. Think of Wilf. He's an old man.'

Arthur Catt heard his daughter, but the words refused to sink in. Instead he tried to plough forwards to reach her, only to be bounced backwards by her foot soldiers.

'Excuse me, sorry, I'm trying to reach my daughter.'

'A likely story, mate,' one man roared back. 'I've heard about you bailiffs. You'll do anything to make your money. Well you ain't getting through. No way, José.'

José? thought Arthur. His name was Arthur. And why didn't the man recognise him? They'd lived on Storey Street since before Kay was born. And it wasn't like he'd hidden himself away for years . . . was it?

Frustrated, Arthur stood back, and looked for a way to reach his daughter. But there were none. It was like trying to penetrate the Great Wall of China with an egg whisk and a stick of celery. He lifted his eyes in despair, noting as he did so the old man Wilf, looking at him from the upstairs window.

He wore a smile on his face, and a look of sheer admiration. Like he couldn't believe what people were doing for him. He then pointed firmly at Kay, his smile growing wider and wider until it threatened to push his ears clean off his head.

It was a reaction that spurred a memory back into Arthur's head, of the conversation he and the old man had had on his doorstep. A conversation he had been only too happy to ignore . . . but it was all coming back to him now.

One day soon you will see her in action, fierce and brave, and when you see her, when you hear her roar, then you'll understand. And you won't feel scared. Not for her, and not for yourself. Not any more.

The words echoed round his head, getting larger and louder with every second. Blimey. It was like the old man had been seeing the future.

Maybe, maybe, he wasn't the doddery old fool Arthur had mistaken him for. I mean, look at Kay now! Look at her! She was still a Catt, but she was more than that, roaring and prowling. She was everything Wilf said she was. She was a mountain lion. *He* might still be scared, but maybe he shouldn't be. If Kay could be this brave, then maybe, just maybe . . .

Back in the crowd, General Kay felt her focus being disturbed. She had her troops to marshal, but there was also her dad to consider. How long would it be before he ended this? Before he found a way of reaching her and hoiking her out for further humiliation? Then what would happen to Wilf?

She searched for Dad on the street, but to her surprise, couldn't spot him anywhere.

She continued to look, body swerving and swelling with the tide, but no matter how hard or wide she looked, nothing.

That was, until she spied a sight that she never thought she would see. Dad was returning – nothing unusual about that.

It's what he was carrying that was unexpected. All Kay could hope was that he was going to use it to help, not hinder her all-important mission.

Dad Gets Roped In

Kay's troops groaned like an antique rocking chair being sat on by an elephant after a sixteen-course meal. It really wasn't easy blocking every centimetre of the house from the bailiffs.

Things didn't look good. In fact, they were in danger of being reduced to a pile of splinters at any second. They needed a saviour, they needed them now, and it seemed highly unlikely to Kay that her dad was going to fit the bill.

He was the only figure in sight who wasn't already part of the struggle, but he was having difficulty making his way down the street due to the HUGE coil of rope he was lugging behind him. It was enormous – long enough, Kay reckoned, to lasso the moon, though she had no idea what he was really going to do with it. She could only hope he wasn't going to use it to tie her up and render her helpless.

On Arthur staggered, sweat bursting across his forehead, until he found a spot in the crowd where there were no bailiffs.

'Kay, let me through,' he gasped. Kay kept her distance, behind the wall of bodies. She didn't want to doubt her dad, but she couldn't risk being dragged away either. It was difficult, impossible even, to mask how torn she felt.

'I promise, Kay, I'm not to going to get in the way. I've clearly done that for way too long. So I'm here to help, if you'll let me. I used to be a bit handy with ropes, remember?'

And like a flash, Kay did remember. She remembered Mum, Dad and her, standing at the top of a mountain, held secure by ropes that Dad had made. She remembered his business, Wildest Dreams, that sold these ropes, how many countries he posted them to, how many mountains they had climbed.

And in that moment, she felt a flash of excitement ignite in her chest, and she could see that her dad felt it too.

'Let him through,' she shouted to her troops, who parted briefly, allowing Dad to pass, before slamming shut as the bailiffs zoomed in.

'Right,' said Dad, dropping the rope to the floor. 'We need a second line of defence. And we need it quick.'

He wasn't wrong. Wherever they looked, they saw tired bodies. Although the rebels continued to shuffle, arm in arm, rebuffing and thwarting the bailiffs, it was only a matter of time until the tide was breached.

'You keep this lot motivated for five more minutes,' Dad said, 'and I'll rig something up that these thugs will need ten A-levels to get past.' He flashed a huge smile, which looked alien on his

face, though it suited him more than his usual worried frown. Then he flipped the traffic cone from Kay's head on to his own.

Now he looked like a plonker, as well as happy.

Off he bustled, dragging one end of the rope to the drainpipe that snaked its way up the corner of Wilf's house. After effortlessly shinning halfway up and tying the rope off, he leapt, cat-like, to the ground, and hoisted the rope over his shoulder.

What happened next was baffling and blinding. Kay had

no idea that her dad could move so quickly. Normally his every step was slow, laboured and nervous, but not now. No way. He covered every centimetre of the front yard, never once bothered by the weight of the rope he was carrying, nor the pressure he was working under.

For the next few minutes he tore around the space, finding railings and poles and pipes to wrap the rope around, before dashing again to the opposite fence. What quickly appeared before their eyes was a gigantic, intricate spider's web, with the rope knotted and pulled so tight that Kay reckoned she could use it as a trampoline.

As he beavered away, climbing high and hanging upside down by his knees, the space between each strand of web got narrower and narrower, and higher and deeper. It would take a team of ninja tarantulas a week to create what her dear old dad had whipped together in four minutes and thirty-two seconds.

Puffed out but happy, he stood before his masterwork.

'Not bad. Forgot I could even do that, never mind how much fun it was.'

'Not bad?' Kay gasped, before throwing herself with abandon into his arms. 'It's amazing!'

But as the pair congratulated each other, there was a creak

and a groan behind them. Those sneaky bailiffs had consolidated their brawn and formed a crude human battering ram, which was now piling its might against their barricade. The adults were taking the full force of the assault, with the kids pushing enthusiastically behind them, but it was no use. Their collective resolve was just too weak, even with Arthur and Kay adding their might.

With one almighty shove, the Storey Street Sea finally parted and the bullies gushed through.

'We've done it!' one yelled.

'We're too strong,' yelled another.

'I have to say, though, they put up a jolly good fight,' said another, who clearly hadn't got the memo about talking only in threatening three-word sentences.

But just as their backslapping was getting out of hand, they spotted the new obstacle in front of them. Some of them looked bemused, others decidedly ticked off, while some merely sneered, mistakenly thinking it was one puny final puzzle to navigate.

The first thug walked up to the web, trying to push his way through it, sneering when his leg passed easily through the first hole. The sneer didn't last long though. It was a replaced by a look of confusion when he realized the hole wasn't quite big

enough to fit the rest of his bulk through. He tried, of course
he did, because his ego was fifteen times the size of his brain.
But every movement just served to make the situation worse,
and before he knew it, he was tangled in the rope's labyrinth,
helpless. Stuck.

Oh, how the other meatheads laughed. What a fool their
colleague was! No way were they going to make the same idiotic
mistakes he did. *They* would be the one to defeat the rope and

kick the helpless old man out of his home.

One by one, they strode forwards, chest puffed out, knuckles cracking in readiness.

One by one, they all ended up in the same ridiculous predicament, flummoxed by the complexity of the web. Some tried to stay low and crawl through, others tried to scale high and crawl over.

Their method was irrelevant: the result was the same. Like lemmings they followed each other, and like total and utter dipsticks, they all fell into the same trap. Twenty-five minutes later, every single one of them was stuck. The front door might have been only metres away, but it might as well have been in Timbuktu. They weren't going to reach it, not today.

They'd be lucky if they managed to wrestle their way free, as strangely enough, the Storey Street residents ignored their desperate pleas for help, choosing instead to pose in front of them for photos, like a mahoosive football team who had just won the World Cup, ten million–nil.

Their celebrations were wild and undiluted; well, until the ice cream man started to play his tune over the loudspeaker. It was a time for a treat, and oh boy, did they deserve one. In fact they deserved a triple cone with flake, hundreds and thousands and every sauce ever invented.

No one was going home hungry. They were going home full, triumphant and . . . sickly.

Which left Kay and Arthur Catt in Wilf's front yard, giggling at the mayhem that they had just created, and the risky, dangerous, downright perilous adventure they had just gone on.

Both were tired – in fact, they were downright bushed. But both wore a smile. And both felt *alive*.

'Shall we go see your friend?' Arthur asked, beckoning to a beaming Wilf in the window.

'Bit risky trying to get through this, isn't it?' said Kay, looking at the rope web.

Arthur gulped hard, swallowing his habit of feeling scared. 'It'll be fine. You go first and I'll follow. I'm sure you'll show me the way.'

Kay needed no more encouragement, and scampered her way up the ropes, steering clear of grasping hands and shaven heads. Only when she reached the summit did she stop and wait for Dad, and the two of them sat there, just for a moment, feeling like they were perched on the top of the world. Dad even pulled out his phone for a quick selfie.

'Race you to the bottom,' Kay giggled.

'No competition,' Dad replied. And down they sped, racing towards Wilf Wilkinson, who was stood on the doorstep, staff in hand, waiting to give them the warmest and most magical hug ever felt in Seacross, or anywhere else for that matter.

27

Happily Ever Afte-

I interrupt this beautiful happy ending, to bring you a reality check.

Because life on Storey Street, contrary to what you might have heard, is not a fairy tale, nor is this one of Aesop's fables.

This is real, written down just as I saw it, and so I have to report that other things happened after that wonderful, heartwarming hug, after Arthur Catt shook Wizard Wilf's hand and apologised for misjudging him so unkindly.

The Catts might have *delayed* the bailiffs in their quest, capturing them like insects in a sticky lair, but eventually, after some fevered phone calls and some very sharp knives, they tumbled gracelessly to the ground to lick their wounds and remember that, although humiliated, they were still owed money.

And they were doubly determined to collect it.

They would be back, it was inevitable, and Kay, Wilf and

Arthur all knew this.

So after warm, proper introductions between the two men, Kay suggested they try and fix Wilf's situation. But that was harder than it sounded.

There is never any point in sticking an Elastoplast on a leg that needs amputating, and as grim as it sounds, that was a fitting analogy for Wilf's financial situation.

He was potless, broke, skint. His bank statements were moth-eaten and instead of containing several zeroes, they listed only one. He had no assets left to sell, and refused point-blank to profit from selling his feline friends, not that it would have solved his debts – far from it.

So the trio sat on upturned boxes and brainstormed a solution.

'Do you have any shares or investments you could cash in?' Wilf's head shook.

'Or inheritance from your wife?'

'She gave it all to cat charities. Who was I to protest?'

'Any family who could offer a loan? Or a roof, even if it's just for a while?'

'Alas, no. It's little old me on my own.'

Arthur pushed himself up from the box, his face stern and

voice matter-of-fact. 'Well there's only one thing for it then, isn't there?'

Kay's heart stalled like a car with a whoopee cushion for an engine. What was he going to say?

There's nothing we can do to help?

Or

I'll reserve you a couple of cardboard boxes under the motorway bridge?

He wouldn't say that, would he? Not after what they'd just been through.

She braced herself, not wanting to hear.

'Wilf will have to come and live with us then, won't he?

An orchestra of party poppers exploded in Kay's head, propelling her into Dad's arms, knocking him over the box and on to his back.

'Just for a while,' he grinned. 'Till he's back on his feet. And there will be rules. Cat-related rules.'

'Rules are good,' Kay beamed. 'We like rules, don't we, Wilf?'

'We do,' said Wilf. 'They're spellbinding.' And his glasses steamed up with gratitude and emotion.

And so it came to pass (I've always wanted to write that) that Wilf Wilkinson left his crumbling old terrace, tucking the key under the doormat for the bailiffs, and walked the hundred metres to the Catt residence, the kittens trailing behind him.

Well, some of the kittens.

One of Dad's rules had been that Wilf found foster homes for seventy-five per cent of them, just until he found his own place, so Kay had knocked on every door in Storey Street on

a re-housing mission: a mission that was surprisingly easy. Many simply wanted to help Wilf out, whilst others remained paranoid about the mice returning and were happy to have a moggie to deter them. Either way, within hours, Kay had met Dad's demands and Wilf was happy. If he played his stereo loud enough, he knew that he could summon the troops and still hold one heck of a disco.

It was the start of a happy time for Kay Catt. Her house was full of many things: laughter, cats, music, magic and friends. Liv and Daisy Smith became regular visitors to her house. People started to joke that the twins had become triplets. It was all most agreeable.

The only thing that had disappeared was something that Kay didn't miss: fear.

It was like Wilf had waved his staff and banished it to a parallel universe.

He performed his own brand of magic on Dad too, persuading him to wind up his safety business and return to his Wildest Dreams.

'Your ropes should be climbing mountains, not languishing in a loft,' Wilf demanded. 'Don't forget, you are no average father. You've raised a mountain lion, so it's time to bare your own teeth. Wouldn't you agree?'

Arthur didn't quite understand, but Wilf was so positive and persistent that it wasn't long before more ropes found themselves snaking out of the attic. Orders came from America and New Zealand, India and Tibet. Wildest Dreams was back in action and Dad was feeling more intrepid than he had in many a year.

And as for Kay? Well, dear reader, you've no reason to worry about her.

She might not have found a bona fide wizard living nearby, but she had something else instead.

Something magical in a different way.

She had the Sorceror of Storey Street living under her roof, and while that was the case?

Anything was possible.

The End . . . sob.

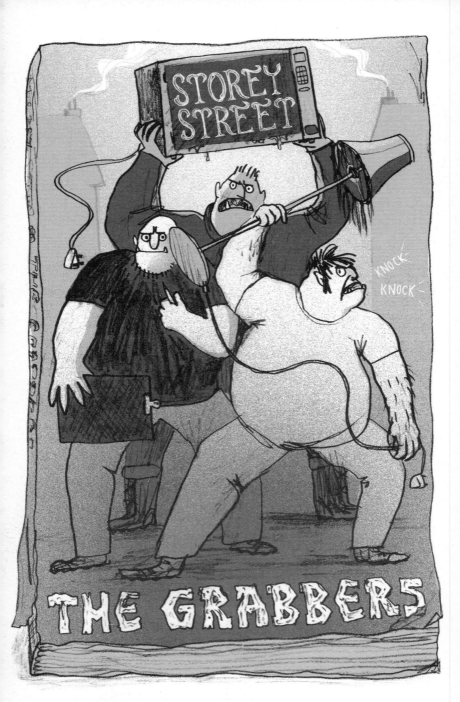

Acknowledgements

Ah, the final thank yous in the final Storey Street book.
Thank you for reading them, if indeed you have. You might just
have picked this up idly in a charity shop to pass a few seconds
while your mum donates your old clothes, especially that unicorn
jumper your great aunt bought you for Christmas. Either way,
thanks (to you, not your aunt, obviously).

I've bloomin' loved writing them, and it's been a thrill
and an honour to get to work with Sara Ogilvie,
who is without doubt my illustrating hero. Thank you Sara.

Thank you also to Stephanie Allen, who is brilliant
at what she does, to Jen Breslin for her unending positivity,
and to Helen Thomas for listening and waiting
and encouraging throughout.

I owe a huge debt to Jodie Hodges as well for being basically,
brilliant, not to mention Mum, Dad, Jon, Kate and Snoop.
Thank you to my friends, in the Bridge and in CP for pushing/
carrying me over the finish line, and to Lou and Nancy for
appearing out of nowhere and plastering a grin the size
of Seacross back onto my face.

Finally, thank you to Albie, Elsie and Stanley.
You are at the heart of every story I'll ever tell.

Hebden Bridge,
July, 2017